Amelia's Gift

DEBRA JOHN

BALBOA.
PRESS
A DIVISION OF HAY HOUSE

Balboa Press books may be ordered through booksellers or by contacting:

Balboa Press
A Division of Hay House
1663 Liberty Drive
Bloomington, IN 47403
www.balboapress.com
1-(877) 407-4847

ISBN: 978-1-4525-4286-7 (sc)
ISBN: 978-1-4525-4288-1 (hc)
ISBN: 978-1-4525-4287-4 (e)

Library of Congress Control Number: 2011961032

Printed in the United States of America

Balboa Press rev. date: 12/02/2011

To my mother Amelia

Acknowledgements

Writing this book has been a phenomenal experience and would not have been possible without the encouragement and support of my family and friends. I am immensely grateful to my sister, Gail Ingson, who has been a true inspiration throughout the entire process, encouraging me every step of the way. I am also thankful for my fiancé, Eugene Symbalisty, who kept me focused on my writing, exclaiming to me many times, "But you have to write it."

Sincere appreciation is extended to those who granted me permission to include them as part of my story: Gordon Smith, John Holland, Gregg Braden, John Rogers, and Hazel West Burley.

I would like to thank the following for their special contributions:

Daniel Sanzone for the magnificent piece of artwork he created for my book cover. As a student at the Savannah College of Art and Design, I know that he will do great things for the world with his talent for art. He already has for me.

Jeanne Beatty for her continued support and valued suggestion that her son Daniel create the artwork for my book cover.

My editor, Julie Johnson, for the many hours that she spent with me so I could provide feedback to her edits as she made them.

Davin Swendsen for his support and encouraging me to write more details into my story.

Barbara Kyle for her valuable feedback to my many questions about writing.

And finally, I would like to thank everyone I worked with during my 34 years with the Department of Defense. They were my true teachers when it came to learning how to write. Especially, I would like to thank the military supervisors who shared their knowledge of the English language and writing prose.

(Prologue)

O N A HOT SUNDAY AFTERNOON in the month of August, Lisa Marie Anderson arrived at Kimbrough Army Hospital to visit her mother Amelia. As she walked with her father Ed toward the hospital entrance, she could not get the vision out of her head—the vision that was now a vivid memory from the day before. When she stood in the front yard, watching her father pull his green Chrysler Imperial out of the driveway, she could see the sadness in her mother's eyes—waving her hand in front of her pale white face, looking through the passenger side window, as if she was waving goodbye for the last time.

Continuing their walk down the long gray hallway, her thoughts turned to the phone call her father received earlier in the day. Devastated and heartbroken, tears filled his eyes when he heard the nurse tell him, "We're so sorry, but we don't expect Amelia to make it through the night." Lisa felt fortunate that she was there to comfort him when he received the news. Her original plans were to visit her parents in July, the week of her 29th birthday. For some reason— perhaps a gut feeling—she switched her flight from Florida to arrive in Maryland during the month of August. It was a touch of fate that she arrived only three days before her mother's stroke, as if she was meant to be there for the last few days of her life.

As they walked into the Intensive Care Unit, they were approached by the nurse. "Hello, my name is Janet. I am the attending nurse and will be keeping watch over Amelia this evening. Before you see her, I need to tell you about her condition. As I told you earlier today, we don't expect her to make it through the night. And because her major organs are now failing, she has slipped into a coma."

Wanting to be alone with his wife, her father went in to see her first. Patiently awaiting her turn to see her mother, Lisa asked the nurse, "Will she be able to hear me if I speak to her—and be able to respond in any way?"

Speaking with a soft voice, she answered her and said, "Because she's in a coma dear, it isn't likely she'll respond to anything that you do or say. But there's a slight chance you may feel a response from her if you hold her hand and ask her to move it."

When her father came out of the room, she could tell he had been crying by the redness in his eyes—evidence of spending final moments with the woman he shared his life with for the past forty years. Struggling with his words, he said to Lisa, "You may go in and see your mother now. This may be the last time you'll ever . . ."

Not being able to say another word, he walked over to the waiting area. As Lisa walked toward the entrance to her mother's room, she slightly turned her head to look back at her father. Sitting in the dingy gray waiting room chair, holding his white handkerchief over his tear-streaked eyes; he was sobbing as she heard him say to himself: "How am I ever going to live without her?"

She walked over to her mother's bedside and sat in the chair next to her bed. Praying that she would somehow receive a response from her, she took the nurse's advice and spoke to her while she held her hand. "Mommy, I know that you can't speak to me . . . but if you can hear me, please squeeze my hand."

Disappointment came over her when she did not feel a response. After a moment or two passed, her mother spoke. As if by a miracle, the words that she spoke were as clear and solid as if she were fully awake.

"I don't know what to do . . . Should I stay here or go there?"

Lisa quickly looked above her mother, expecting to see an angel from Heaven that may have prompted her to speak. She then looked back at her mother and spoke purely from her heart—the first and only words she ever meant with every fiber of her being.

"Mommy, we love you very much and we'll miss you . . . but you have been in a lot of pain lately. I think you'll be much happier if you go to Heaven."

The next morning the nurse called and said she had passed peacefully during the night, but before she could slip into eternal slumber, she had a smile on her face and was singing a song. It was one of her favorites, written by the youngest of her six children, Mark.

For the next twenty-four years, Lisa often relived this story and told it many times. Every time that she did, it caused her to cry. Many times she prayed at night, asking God if she could hear from her. All she wanted to know was that she was OK. She loved her dearly and missed her terribly. Twenty-four years later her prayers were answered—with a profound message from above. This message set into motion a chain of events that miraculously changed her life for the better. This is her story.

─────(Chapter 1)─────

AFTER MY MOTHER'S FUNERAL, I returned to my home in Cape Canaveral, Florida. Even though my apartment was small and had only one bedroom, the location made it absolutely perfect for me. The beach was so close that I could walk to it within a matter of minutes. Most days I enjoyed walking on the beach, feeling the warmth of the sun on my face, listening to the gentle roar of the waves washing ashore, smelling the salt spray, and looking out upon the horizon with its white puffy clouds. On days when the waves pounded the shore with a thunderous roar, and I felt adventurous, I took my boogie board to the beach. Besides being loads of fun, it was a great way to stay in shape. As I held onto my board, I first had to jump through the crashing waves until I made it past the break point. When the perfect wave was upon me, cresting with its clear wall of water, I jumped onto my board, as if jumping onto a sled. While kicking my feet and paddling my hands at a furious pace, my board and I were lifted by the wave. It was an exhilarating ride back to the shore as I felt the speed of the wave, tasted the ocean water splashing my face, and heard the sound of sand scraping my board as I came to a sudden stop on the beach. I would then stand up and do it all over again.

Because the beach was only a few miles from Cape Canaveral Air Force Station, and I could see the launch complexes, I was able to watch the entire launch sequence from the ground up. Each time that a rocket blasted off from the launch pad, and then soared into the clouds, it created a tremendous crackling sound that became louder and louder as the winds brought it closer to me. If a rocket launched during the night while I was sleeping, the sound of windows rattling in my apartment was loud enough to awaken me from a deep sleep. Local residents, who had lived there since the Apollo launches to the moon, told me the vibrations from those launches were so intense that they cracked windows in cars and houses. Life was exciting on the Space Coast of Florida.

Shortly after I had relocated to my new home in paradise in 1980, I received a beautiful handwritten letter from my mother. The letter was written not long after her second heart attack, and two years before her stroke. At the time that she wrote the letter, my younger brother Mark was at the beginning of his singing career. My younger sister Dottie had just graduated with her Master's Degree and was looking for her first job at a bank on Long Island. My two older brothers were working full-time. My brother Billy was teaching art at one of the county middle schools, and my oldest brother Daniel was working for a computer company in England. My older sister Gail was living in another town with her husband Phil and her two children, Paul and Valerie:

Dearest Lisa -

We received your lovely letter and it seems you have finally found your end of the rainbow. I am so happy for you dear. Mark and Bill are all enthused about flying down there this summer and having a good time. I'm sure they will love it there when they visit you. You seem to be located right in the middle of all the clubs, shops, etc.

It's still cold up here and we can't get out to do much. I'll be glad when I can sit outside again. I'm still quite thin, 124 lbs, but at least I don't have any more swelling in my feet. I doubt if I'll be able to make any more trips. I still go to Bingo on Monday and take it easy at home.

Dad feels pretty good and is anxious to get out in his garden.

Dottie is home but she is waiting to hear about a job in New York City. Her friend from college has a job up there and they have put a deposit on an apartment for $625 a month. It has no furniture or even a rug on the floor. We loaned her the money but she'd better get a job soon. Her girlfriend has a chair and dishes. I think they are going to be stuck.

When you go to the Space Shuttle launch, don't forget to take some pictures. That should be very exciting. I know that Mark and Bill would love to see the Space Center. Mark is just starting to get enough jobs to get ahead. Next month will be a full one for him. His singing is getting better and better and everyone loves him. Daniel has been in England but will be home in a few days to visit for a week. Gail still comes by and asks about you. Everyone is happy for you dear.

Well dear, I don't have any more news so I'll close for now. Send some of your sunshine up here.

All our love,
Mom, Dad & Family
xxx

Returning to my normal routine after losing my mother was not easy for me. I missed hearing the sweet sound of her voice on the phone and being able to have conversations with her. She was always there for me when I needed advice or someone to chat with.

Although I felt great sadness from losing her, I also felt extreme comfort in knowing that she was in Heaven. The words that she spoke to me—from her hospital bed—were all the evidence that I needed. Hearing her words reassured my belief that there is much more to our existence than our presence here on earth. Having my own piece of evidence that she was in Heaven also made the grieving process easier for me. It allowed me to keep my focus on the light of Heaven instead of the darkness of death.

When I used to call her, my father sometimes talked on the phone, but only long enough to say hello or to ask how I was. Because he had a habit of not talking much to his children, my conversations with him were always short and to the point. My brothers and sisters and I were always close to our mother, but it was not the same when it came to our relationship with our father. After fighting in World War II and the Korean War, he decided not to become close to his children. The reason he often gave us was that he did not want us to miss him when he died. Another reason that he gave had to do with something that happened to him as a child. His father always favored his younger brother over him, which caused him to feel unloved and unwanted. Not wanting the same thing to happen to his own children, he chose not to have any favorites. He achieved this goal by not spending too much time with any of us.

Since he was the only person that I could speak to when I called home, my conversations with him were better than before. Instead of just saying hello, he was more open to my sharing things with him about my personal life. The only problem was that I had to call him early enough in the day—before he began drinking alcohol. According to my brothers and sisters, who still lived in Maryland, he had become even more difficult to live with since my mother died. He loved her dearly and found life difficult without her. Instead of asking those who loved and cared for him to help him through the healing process, he turned to alcohol for help. Because he was drinking more often than he used to, his drinking habit became worse with each day. It was his way of dealing with the emotional pain that came with losing someone near and dear to his heart. My older sister Gail sent me a letter during this time that describes how his personality changed for the worse since the death of my mother. This is a short excerpt from her letter:

> *I call Dad every day during the morning. He's all right then but has started getting drunk every night and back to his old mean self. He threatened to disinherit Mark because he didn't come cut the grass in 100 degree weather, and to disinherit Bill because he would not come pick him and the car up at the Elks Lodge. He hasn't started on me yet but I expect him to eventually. If he keeps it up he will drive all of us away from him and he won't have anyone.*

Because my grandfathers died before I was born, I had only grandmothers while I was growing up. My paternal grandfather, whose name was Joseph, lived from 1883 to 1942. During the prohibition era in the 1920s, he and my Grandmother Mary ran a bathtub still operation in their basement. It was a pretty common thing in the state of New York during that time, along with bootleggers, speakeasies, moonshine, and rum runners who smuggled supplies of alcohol from Canada across state lines. On more than a few occasions, my father and his mother had some heated discussions about her home-based operation—usually prompted by her complaints about his drinking habit.

My father would become angry with her, defending himself by saying things like: "Don't you dare criticize me for my drinking! When I was just a young boy, don't you remember keeping me home from school to help you put caps on your liquor bottles? And did you forget about the speakeasies you used to have all the time?"

Whenever I heard some of these arguments about bathtub stills and speakeasies, it made me wonder whether or not my grandmother was a wild woman in her younger days. She lived with my parents throughout their entire marriage, except for the few years that they lived in Frankfurt, Germany. She was an intelligent woman who was sweet and loving toward the children. Because my father was in the military, he asked her to live with us so she could help my mother with the children while he was away. I always had the impression from my mother that she wasn't too thrilled with this living arrangement.

She told me several times while I was growing up: "When you get married, don't ever let your mother-in-law live with you. If you do, she'll try to run your life for you." My mother was always giving me advice. She was never afraid to speak her mind about any topic.

My maternal grandfather, whose name was Arthur, lived from 1891 to 1934. He died from a stroke when my mother was only 18 years old, leaving my Grandmother Maria with very little money to support the family. To help out with family finances, my mother had to work a full-time job. She worked in the Electronic Tube Department at the General Electric Company in her home town of Schenectady, New York. In 1941, a photo of her working on the assembly line was featured on the front cover of their *Factory* magazine. They chose her for the photo shoot because of her natural beauty and the colorful apron that she was wearing that day. In the photo, she had naturally curly brown hair, but as a young girl her hair was blonde. She also had a fair complexion and hazel eyes. Because my mother was athletic, she was chosen to play on the company's basketball team. In the summer months, she worked part-time as a lifeguard.

Before meeting my father, my mother met a man named Daniel. They worked together for four years at the General Electric Company. Tall, blonde, and handsome, he was an extremely intelligent electrical engineer with dreams of starting his own company. She talked about him often while I was growing up, telling me how they went skiing together in the mountains of New York and how much they loved each other. He turned out to be who she referred to as "the love of her life." She was heartbroken when he had to move to California to start his own business and then quickly married another woman. When they could no longer see each other, she promised to name her firstborn son after him. In a nutshell, he was the man she could never have but always wanted. My mother met my father two years after Daniel moved to California. Although she loved my father, she often told me that the happiest years of her life were those that she spent with Daniel.

My parents met when my mother was playing a pinball machine. When I was growing up, I remember her joking about winning him as her prize for playing the game. When my father proposed to my mother, he was serving with the US military as a 1st Sergeant. The ring that he gave her had a quarter carat natural blue diamond—a remarkable stone so rare that most jewelers today have never seen one. He paid for the ring with fifty dollars that he won at a poker tournament. He loved to gamble, and so did my mother. Whenever she had a few nickels to spare, she walked two blocks to the local drugstore where she played the mechanical slot machines. Occasionally, she won the big jackpot and came home with ten dollars worth of nickels in her pocketbook. She also loved to play bingo at the Elks Lodge and the Moose Lodge. She was lucky at bingo and won most of the time when she went. When I became old enough to play, I went to the bingo halls with her, even though the dense cloud of smoke in the room caused my eyes to sting and water. When I watched the other women in the room, I could never figure out why they had to smoke like chimneys while they played the game.

My mother told me the reason she married my father was because he was fun to hang around with and he had a love for music. He played the piano, the banjo, and the accordion. He was also tall and handsome. With his jet black hair and well-trimmed mustache, he was a spitting image of Errol Flynn. According to my father, he married my mother because she was beautiful and she loved to dance like he did. He often bragged about her athletic abilities and how she was the star player on the General Electric basketball team. Evidence of my father's love for my mother is reflected in a beautiful poem he wrote to her a year after they were married. It was written during the time that he was fighting in Northern France under General Patton during the Second World War. He was a member of the Fourth Armored Infantry Division. When my mother received the letter, she had just given birth to their first child together, my sister Gail.

It's just a year ago today
That you and I were wed
And when you asked if I loved you
This is what I said.

I love you madly darling
But I'm jealous as can be
Do you think that you can always
Look at no one else but me?

And from the answer you gave me
Twas plain as plain could be
That you cared nothing for anyone else
Your love was all for me.

So life goes on and here we are
Three thousand miles apart
How in the world can you ever know
The things that are in my heart.

In the morning when I wake dear
My first thought is of you
I wonder where you are today
And what you'll have to do.

Then at noon I'm thinking of you
When the sun is way up bright
And I think she's had her breakfast now
Wonder what she'll do tonight.

Then at night as I sit here so lonely
Wishing that you were here
A grand warm feeling comes over me
And I'm sure that you are near

I may not be able to see you
Nor actually hear what you say
But I know you're here beside me
And have been all through the day.

Your appreciative husband
Ed

Portions of another letter, which my father wrote to my mother, were quoted in a local Schenectady newspaper. As published in the newspaper article titled, "Local Soldier Captures 8 Germans," this is his humble account of his experience. He wrote the letter using paper and a typewriter left behind by hastily departing Nazis.

I've taken quite a few prisoners—eight alone and the rest with a lot of help. The bunch I took were pointed out to me by a Frenchman. They were sleeping under a tree behind a cemetery. I kicked one of them and they all jumped up with their hands in the air. Guess they were waiting for someone to surrender to anyway, so there was nothing to it.

As a child growing up, I looked at my father as someone who was mean and difficult to live with. When I became older and realized what he had to live through during the war, I came to understand why he drank alcohol. It was his way of melting away the traumatic memories from fighting in the war. Knowing this, I was also able to forgive him for how he treated me while I was growing up. After my father died, my sister Gail gathered up all the family history records. She showed me a newspaper article published in the *Schenectady Union-Star* with quotes from my father. The article is titled, "Comical Experiences, Not Funny at the Time, Says GI." When I read the article, it showed me a side of him that I never knew existed when I was a child. I was utterly amazed and extremely proud that he was able to maintain his sense of humor amongst all the horror that comes with war. These are some of his comical experiences from the war:

When a person has a little time to sit back and think, there are a lot of funny things that happen during the war—things that don't seem funny while they're happening.

One of the most amusing incidents relates to a time when I was searching a building in Normandy for booby traps. I heard someone in one of the rooms, and sneaked up to the door and kicked it open, with my rifle ready. The next thing I knew—I was flat on my back. A scared pig ran out, right between my legs. That animal couldn't have scared me any more if it had been a German tank.

Another time, I was caught under a barrage of artillery, while operating the radio in my half-track. Seven shells in a row threw mud in the track, and over 25 of them hit in a circle within 75 yards. I really learned a lot of new prayers during that session.

After one of my men dug a foxhole which I thought was too small, I bawled him out by telling him it wasn't big enough for a midget. At that moment, a shell came winning over, and a few seconds later, I looked around and we were both in the hole—with plenty of room to spare.

While on the topic of foxholes, I must tell you about another experience with one. I dug a honey—put a good heavy roof on it and crawled in for the night. A couple of hours later, I woke up blowing bubbles in the water. It seemed that in the sector we were in, you only had to go down a foot to strike water. I slept on top of

*the ground that night. Forget the shells—I'd rather be
shot than drowned.*

Life wasn't always easy or funny for my father when he was
fighting in the war. When he received a shrapnel wound to his leg,
he received the prestigious Purple Heart Medal—a United States
military decoration, awarded in the name of the president to those
who have been wounded or killed while serving.

─────────────(Chapter 2)─────────────

AFTER TWO WARS AND SEVERAL years of serving with the military, my father retired and began his new life as a civilian. He was employed as a government employee with the National Security Agency at Fort Meade, Maryland. The family moved out of military housing and moved into a two-story house in the suburbs just south of Baltimore. My father bought the house for $17,000. Located in a nice neighborhood, it was at the end of a street in what we referred to as "The Circle," formally known as a cul-de-sac. All six children lived in this house until they married, joined the service, or in my situation, just decided to move out. The house had green aluminum siding and a gray shingle roof. There were two bedrooms on the first floor and three on the second floor. On the first floor, my parents lived in the first bedroom and my Grandmother Mary lived in the second bedroom. The children lived on the second floor, with various room arrangements as we grew up. Every house in the neighborhood was built with the same floor plan, but some of them were modified by their owners. We were lucky that ours had been modified with a room addition at the back of the house, which we called the family room. This is the room where we spent most of our time together, usually watching television. The children normally sat on the brown vinyl sofa while our parents sat in the two recliners. Whenever our father wasn't in his recliner, the children enjoyed sitting in it and searching for money that fell out of his pockets.

The family room had wood paneling on the walls and large windows that looked out into the backyard. In the backyard, we had a shed that my older brothers Daniel and Billy built. And we also had a garden. My father's garden provided some of my fondest memories while growing up, except for the times when I had to help him pull the weeds. He loved being outside and working in the garden—growing all sorts of fruits and vegetables like lettuce, corn, green and red peppers, tomatoes, carrots, and strawberries. Before spring arrived, my father utilized the large windows in our family room to create his own greenhouse. He first planted seeds in small pots, put plastic bags over the pots, and then placed them on the window sills. By the time spring arrived, the plants were ready to be planted in our garden. When the plants matured and the fruits and vegetables were ripe for harvest, I was the first to pick them. There is nothing better than eating vegetables right after they are picked. My favorite was always tomatoes, plucking them from the vine, smelling their sweet fragrance, savoring their flavor with each delicious bite that I took. In the wintertime, when the garden was covered with snow, we sat in front of the wood fireplace while we watched television.

Television being quite different in the early sixties, there were no channel changers—unless you want to call the children that—and there were only three channels to choose from (ABC, CBS and NBC). We were fortunate that the family could afford to own a color television, and only because my father saved money by building it from a kit. When he retired from the government, he used government funds, available for continuing education, and enrolled with Heathkit—an electronic kit company located in St Joseph, Michigan. Over the span of a few years, he received several kits through the mail. Each kit contained detailed, non-technical instructions with large diagrams, taking my father through each step, showing him exactly what to do and how to do it. Because the government paid for the course, and the kits were included, it allowed our family to have some pretty cool electronics that we normally could not afford. In addition to the color television, he built a microwave oven, a trash compacter, and a few other household electronics.

Back in those days, watching television in the evenings was considered a family event. Since most households had only one television set, everyone had to watch the same show together. We especially looked forward to Saturday nights when we watched NBC's *Saturday Night at the Movies*. Another favorite weekly show was *Walt Disney's Wonderful World of Color*. Occasionally, we had special programs to watch such as *The Wizard of Oz*. Special shows like this gave us something to look forward to each year when they aired on their yearly anniversary. My favorite as a little girl was *Rogers and Hammerstein's Cinderella*. On Saturday mornings, us kids were able to choose the programs we wanted because our parents were still sleeping. My all-time favorite cartoon program was *Casper the Friendly Ghost*.

Another activity that I enjoyed doing in the family room was listening to music on a set of headphones. As I sat in my father's favorite recliner, I played all my favorite records from the 1960s, sometimes for hours at a time. The first record that I ever bought was *Build Me Up Buttercup* by the Foundations. Other records that I bought and loved to listen to were *My Special Angel, Till, and Turn Around Look at Me* by the Vogues. From the time that I was a young child until now, I have always had a deep appreciation for music—with a firm belief that listening to music is one of the closest things to Heaven that we have here on earth, second only to the emotional joys of being in love.

Since our house was in a cul-de-sac, the kids in our neighborhood were able to play in the street without worrying about cars in the road. Softball, kickball, dodge ball—these were the games most popular for kids at that time. Other games that we played, which required less physical activity and more strategy, were kick-the-can and hide-and-seek. Being easier to hide when it is dark outside, we always played hide-and-seek or kick-the-can after the sun went down. Since our parents made us stay inside the house after dark, I had to climb out of my bedroom window from the second floor if I wanted to play games when it was dark outside. The boy that lived next door was my favorite companion for playing games. His name was Bill and his parents made sure that he was involved in all sorts of sports when he was growing up. He was such a good athlete that he became a professional football player after graduating from the University of South Carolina. He was drafted by the Houston Oilers in the early seventies and later on played for the New York Giants. He retired one year before the Giants won the super bowl.

The housing community that we lived in had a community center to which our family had a membership. The membership gave us unlimited access to an Olympic-sized swimming pool, and also a beautiful lake that was perfect for water skiing in the summer and ice skating in the winter. When we walked to the pool, our path took us down a long rocky road. Since we were barefooted most of the time when we played outdoors, we seldom wore shoes—even when we walked down the rocky road to the pool. After several weeks, our feet toughened up enough that we were able to walk on the rocks without feeling them digging into the bottom of our feet. One of my favorite things to do in my bare feet was running through the puddles in the street after a rainstorm. A hilarious memory, which I shall never forget, happened one day while I was visiting the community pool with my two sisters, Gail and Dottie. While we were sitting on our towels getting ready to go swimming, we noticed a group of women we had not seen before. When they arrived, we could tell by their actions that they were not from the local community. We watched them with intense curiosity as they carefully placed their towels on the ground, and then removed all their clothing so that they could put their bathing suits on, as if it were the normal thing to do. My older sister Gail had to explain to my younger sister Dottie and me that they were probably from another country where the customs were not the same as ours.

Overall, growing up with five brothers and sisters created many special memories—most of which I will treasure for a lifetime. There are many other memories, however, that I wish I could forget. Although I give my father a lot of credit for being an excellent provider, keeping a roof over our heads and food on the table—his love for alcohol made life difficult for everyone living in the same house with him. Many nights he came home drunk after boozing with the guys he worked with, frequenting places like the Elks Lodge, the Moose Lodge, or any other bar named after an animal. Depending on what he had to drink that night and how much, his personality often changed for the worse, turning him into a mean and nasty person. We felt fortunate that even though he hurt us emotionally many times, calling us names and accusing us of doing things we never did—he never hurt us physically—although he did on occasion yank his belt off his trousers and wave it at us to get our attention when he was angry with us.

He told me many years later that hanging out with the guys and drinking was just how it was back then—and it was the mother's role to stay at home and nurture the children. This routine may have worked early on in my parent's marriage; however, things changed after a serious injury to his head. The children never knew what really caused my father's injury. His version of the story was that he was injured while on duty with the military; however, my mother's version was that he fell off a bar stool because he was drunk. I never knew which one of them to believe. His injury required a metal plate to be surgically placed inside his head. As a result of this injury, the doctor prescribed him Phenobarbital in order to prevent seizures. Unfortunately, the medication did not mix well with liquor. If he drank an alcoholic beverage that contained liquor, the result was a drastic change to his personality for the worse.

I remember my mother telling me many times, "As long as your father drinks only beer he's fine, but once he drinks anything with whiskey in it he becomes mean and nasty and he can turn on you like a snake."

On a more positive note, my mother, Amelia, had a kind and nurturing disposition, giving us all the love and affection that we needed—always putting us first. Even though she did not have much time to herself, I do not remember her ever being sick while I was growing up.

She used to tell us: "Mommies don't have time to be sick. We have to stay healthy so we can take care of our children."

Looking more like her than I do my father, I inherited my mother's curly blonde hair. In my earliest memories, my mother's hair had already turned gray—a beautiful silver color. Her hairdresser never colored her hair, telling her it was a color that other customers often asked for. My mother also had a gorgeous peach complexion which did not require a lot of makeup. Whenever she and my father went out to a special event, the only makeup that she put on was lipstick and then some blush on her cheeks.

My father often told us: "One of the reasons I married your mother is because she always looked as beautiful in the morning as she did the night before."

Adding to this statement, he constantly reminded his three daughters, "When you girls get older, there will be no need to wear a lot of war paint on your faces."

Having six children, and having to raise them on a military income, took its toll on my mother. After she gave birth to her fifth child, she started gaining weight and eventually became obese. Even though I knew she was overweight, it did not bother me as a child. Always a loving and compassionate woman, she hugged her children all the time.

Sometimes when she hugged me I would tell her: "Mommy, I feel bad for the other kids in school with skinny mommies. They don't have as much mommy to hug."

My father fought with my mother many times in the evenings. It was usually after he had a few drinks with the guys before he came home. As a small child, I was frightened at times when I heard my parents yelling at each other. I always worried that my father would hit my mother and possibly hurt her if he became too angry. During one of their arguments, he became so angry that he ripped the phone right off the wall, taking part of the wall with it, leaving behind a gaping hole with wires sticking out where the phone used to be. All she had done was talk to her mother for a few minutes using long distance minutes that he had to pay for. Another time she locked the bedroom door as an attempt to keep him out of the room so that she would be safe from him. In a rage of drunken anger, he put his fist right through the door—enabling him to open it and continue fighting with her.

Another incident happened during the middle of the week when the entire family was waiting for my father to come home for dinner. Although I laugh when I think about it now, it wasn't quite as funny when it happened. When my father came home late for dinner, it was only a few minutes after my mother had placed all the food on the dining room table—the entire family eager to eat what she had spent hours in the kitchen preparing. His excuse for being late had something to do with learning a magic trick with a gentleman at the bar. After grabbing the dining room tablecloth and jerking it off the table—dishes and food crashing to the kitchen floor—he just stood there with a puzzled look on his face, explaining to us that he had just seen a magician do the same trick but with much better results.

When my father became sober the next day, he did not remember doing any of these things—asking us questions like: "Why is there a hole in the bedroom door?" or "Why is the phone ripped off the wall?"

My brother Daniel once used a tape recorder to record my father's voice while my father was drinking. Hoping to make my father realize how bad he was, he tried to play the tape for him the following morning. When he did, my father refused to listen to the tape and then destroyed it.

Occasionally, I heard my parents fighting over Daniel, the man my mother dated before she met my father. She would throw it in my father's face that he would never measure up to Daniel, causing my father to become angry with her. After fighting over my mother's boyfriend for most of their marriage, my father did eventually come to accept her undying love for this man. During one of Daniel's business trips to the Washington DC area, he called my mother on the phone. He wanted to know if she would have lunch with him and offered to send a limousine to the house to pick her up. My father thought it was a great idea, and even encouraged her to go. Ashamed that she had gained too much weight over the years, she turned down the chance of seeing the man she had loved for most of her life. She told us that she wanted him to remember her how she was when they were young and in love.

There were many evenings when my father took the children with him to the local bars. If we were lucky enough to go to the Elks Lodge, there were usually family events that we participated in, or games that we played. My favorite game was table shuffleboard. Since I was competitive as a child, I enjoyed challenging my brothers to a shuffleboard match on occasion, smirking at them whenever my score was higher than theirs—only to be disappointed when they knocked all my pucks off the board during their last turn. There were other times, however, when there were no activities to keep us busy or games to play.

During those times, my father made my brothers and sisters and I sit with our mother in a dark and dreary smoky bar, waiting for several hours for him to finish drinking—listening to him say over and over again, "Just one more drink and we'll all go home."

One more drink always turned into several more drinks, which made the wait even longer. My mother drank alcoholic beverages along with my father, which eventually created an addiction for her as well. When she drank, she always spoke whatever was on her mind, which was sometimes humorous and entertaining. Even though she became a little embarrassing to be with when she drank, she never said anything to anyone that was mean. Most of the time I think my mother drank alcohol because it took away the sadness that she felt—sadness created by how my father treated her. To add to an already bad situation, my father sometimes had nightmares, dreaming about fighting in the war, defending himself by killing the enemy. The dreams were so real at times that he thought my mother was the enemy, waking her up suddenly by trying to choke her in the middle of the night.

Although my father had a serious drinking problem, he never let it interfere with his government job. How he ever managed to make it to work the next morning after he drank—and still function—is something that will always boggle my imagination. Because he had such a high security clearance where he worked, we never knew what his job was. Sometimes he made jokes with us about the new employees. He told us they had to sit in a room and count paper clips until they received their security clearances. While my father worked at the office during the day, my mother worked at home taking care of the children and making preparations for dinner. Preparing our dinner was a daily routine for her, always using fresh ingredients and everything from scratch. She was an excellent cook, turning everyday meat and potatoes into gourmet dishes. She spent hours each day in the kitchen, making everything from chicken and dumplings to homemade Maryland crab cakes. No matter which room of the house I went into, I always smelled something good cooking, making me curious about what we were having for dinner that night. The food that she prepared tasted so good that I could never eat enough of it. At the dinner table each night, I always ate my food faster than anyone else did. That way I knew that I would have seconds. The good thing was, even though I loved to eat, I was still skinnier than any of my brothers and sisters; perhaps because I burned lots of calories by playing outdoors as much as I did. My father often commented on my eating habits while we were sitting at the dinner table.

"Lisa, you must either have a tapeworm or a bottomless stomach. There's no way a young child your size can possibly eat as much as you do."

Sometimes on the weekends, my father took over the kitchen and prepared the family dinner. One of his favorites was lemon-basted chicken cooked on the grill. Maryland steamed crabs, seasoned with Old Bay Seasoning, was another favorite of his, and most definitely the rest of the family. He also prepared a traditional clam bake dinner on occasion. He loved to brag and talk about how he was the one who taught my mother how to cook, but she always disagreed with him when he brought it up. Now that I think about it, there weren't too many things that they did agree on, which was probably one of the reasons why they fought all the time.

There were many things that my mother wanted to buy for her children, but she never had enough money to buy them. In order to have more money to spend on us, she had to be creative. One example of her creativity is the way that she cashed checks from my father's checking account. And she did it without letting him know that she did. When the envelope arrived in the mail with the bank statements, she boiled a pot of water on the stove, held the envelope over the steam, and then opened the envelope without tearing it. She then removed the cancelled checks she had written and resealed the envelope. When my father came home from work later that day, he opened the same envelope to balance his checkbook.

Many times I heard him complaining, as he sat at his desk going through his bank statements, saying to himself: "I don't understand why I can never balance my checkbook. Why don't these figures ever add up?" Even though I knew why he could never balance his checkbook, I just kept quiet, knowing that my mother did it as a means to buy things for her children.

When school started each year in September, my father gave my mother only a few dollars to spend on school supplies and clothing, always telling her, "This should be enough for the kids to get started for the new school year."

The problem was that all he ever gave my mother was enough to get us started, making it difficult when we needed supplies or clothing later in the school year.

I had the courage once to tell my father, "Daddy, if you didn't spend so much money on smoking and drinking, you'd have a lot more money to spend on us kids for clothes and school supplies."

His response to me was not want I wanted to hear. "Lisa, don't ever say that to me again! Those are things I enjoy and deserve. And I'll never give them up."

When my mother shopped for groceries, my father gave her only enough money to buy the essentials, so we seldom had snacks to eat. When we were lucky enough to have a snack, my sister Gail had to do things like divide up the bag of Utz potato chips and give each of us only a few on a napkin. When I received my napkin full of chips, I took my time with eating them, savoring the flavor of each chip, one by one, slowly chewing them in my mouth. Being deprived as a child, by not getting enough potato chips to eat, may be the reason why I now find it difficult to stop eating potato chips whenever I have them; making me think that perhaps a lot of our eating habits could be the result of something we did as a child.

As time went on and the financial situation improved for the family, my father took us on family vacations. After purchasing a tent and all the necessary camping supplies, we began visiting the available parks throughout the state of Maryland. Loving the outdoors as much as I did, I really enjoyed going camping. Our first family camping excursion was to Assateague State Park which was on the Maryland side of Assateague Island. When we set up camp, we pitched our tents right in the sand on the beach. My sister Dottie and I shared a small pup tent, separate from the rest of the family who stayed in one large tent. The sand was pristine white and felt like sugar when we sifted it through our fingers. During the day, we swam in the ocean and worked on our tans. In the evenings, we walked the beach with new friends that we met at the campgrounds. We searched for sand crabs, which came out only at night, and shined our flashlights on them as they skirted across the sand near the water's edge. During this camping trip was when I developed my great love for the ocean and being on the beach. Even today when I go to the beach, I experience a feeling of peace and tranquility that always gives me a sense of being closer to God.

On other camping trips we went to Elk Neck State Park in northern Maryland, and Catoctin Mountain Park in northwestern Maryland. When we camped at Elk Neck State Park, my favorite thing was playing on the Tarzan swing. Made from a thick rope with a large knot at the bottom, it was attached to a large tree in the middle of a deep ravine. It was an exhilarating feeling each time I sat on the knot at the end of the rope, flying through the air like a bird, feeling the wind in my hair, ending the ride when I landed on the other side of the ravine. And then I had to repeat the ride in order to bring the rope back to the other side of the ravine. I also loved doing things like walking through the trails in the woods as I looked for wild deer, or throwing small stones into the stream as I watched them skip across the water.

What I loved most about Catoctin Mountain Park was breathing in the fresh mountain air. Located within the mountainous area known as the Blue Ridge Province, the park was close to one of the Presidential retreats, Camp David. I enjoyed walking several of the nature trails in the park with my two older brothers, Billy and Daniel. Some of the trails led us to visually-stunning rock formations, and others led us to an overlook where we could see other parts of the park or nearby towns in the valley. I was able to overcome my fear of heights after walking these trails. Each one of them led us to an overlook where we looked down and saw views that were often over a thousand feet below us.

By hanging out with my two older brothers while I was growing up, I became quite the tomboy. I loved climbing trees and helping my brothers to build tree houses. When we played in the woods near our house, they enjoyed playing tricks on me. One of the tricks that they were quite good at was setting traps for me in the woods. They created these traps by first digging a hole in the ground that was usually a foot or two in depth, and large enough to cause me to fall into it without being injured. Once they determined that the hole was big enough, they placed branches and twigs over it, and then put newspapers on top of the branches. To finish the trap, they added dirt, leaves, and other debris that they found in the woods. Later on, when my mother told me I could go outside and play with my brothers, I walked into the woods looking for them, clueless about the trap that had just been set for me. After I fell helplessly into their trap, my brothers just stood there and laughed at me hysterically. Luckily, I never received any injuries from falling into the holes that they dug, but was upset and embarrassed each time that it happened. I did figure it out after a few times, walking toward the spot where the dirt was piled up, avoiding the trap—at least until they tricked me again by piling the dirt on top of the trap.

Having five brothers and sisters made my life fun and interesting while I was growing up. Most of the time it was pretty good, except for the evenings that we spent at the bars with our father, or when we had to listen to his war stories after he had been drinking. My father was always filled with emotion when he drank and became extremely talkative. I can remember many school nights listening to him, for what seemed like hours, while he sat on the edge of my bed and told me horrific war stories. He went into great detail on what it was like doing hand-to-hand combat with enemy soldiers—making me feel as if I were in the foxhole with him, fighting during the war. Sometimes it was difficult to wake up for school the next morning because he kept me up so late the night before.

Always trying to see the good side of things, I firmly believe that putting up with my father for all those years, and listening to him for many long hours, is why today I am a strong, patient, and tolerant adult—only because I had to be as a child.

Even though my father was difficult to live with most of the time, there were also good things that he did for the children. The best gift that he ever gave me—which I will always be thankful for—is the gift of music. When I was eight years old, he purchased a brand new Wurlitzer upright piano for the family and paid for me to take piano lessons. I felt privileged that he chose me over my brothers and sisters to learn to play the piano. He told me that he picked me because I had long beautiful fingers that could reach all the piano keys. Once I learned to play fairly well, my older brother Billy sang along with me while I played songs like *Ebb Tide* or *God Bless America*. Although he had an excellent singing voice, it was my younger brother Mark who eventually became a professional singer and musician. He was also given the gift of music by my father when he learned how to play the guitar and the harmonica. It touched my heart in a special way when the nurse told us that my mother was singing one of Mark's songs right before she passed.

─────────────(Chapter 3)─────────────

As the time came closer to my high school graduation, I had to decide where I wanted to work. My father encouraged me to apply for a government job as a secretary, working under the civil service system. Working for the government himself, he realized the many benefits and wanted the same for me—vacation time, sick leave, health insurance, and a great retirement plan. When representatives from the US Government came to our high school to give the civil service exam, I took it and passed with flying colors. A month after I graduated from high school, I was offered a secretarial position working for the US Army at Fort Meade, Maryland.

That was an exciting day for me, and the start of my government career. It wasn't the job I had dreamed about as a child, but the benefits were excellent. My biggest dream was to become a scientist when I grew up. Having a creative mind as a young child, I wanted a career where I could make important scientific discoveries that would make a difference in the world. Another career that I dreamed about was working as a writer. When I was in elementary school, I wrote stories in the classroom while I was sitting at my desk. Creating them in the form of comic strips, they were stories about young women who had adventures and were always rescued by a handsome prince. Before I shared any of my stories with my classmates, I added the comments "To be Continued . . ." at the end of the comic strip, keeping them in suspense until I continued the story the next day.

For my first job, I worked with the 1st Army Headquarters Engineering Department. Sitting behind a gray metal desk, I spent most of the day typing documents for several Army engineers. Typewriters back then did not have any correction keys. If a mistake was made when I typed a letter, I had to either erase it or white it out. In addition to correcting the paper copy, I also had to correct the five or six carbon copies behind it. If I typed a letter for the general's signature, no mistakes or corrections were allowed. When the general received typewritten letters, he held them up to the light to make sure that there were no errors. My father used to tell me, "Whatever the general wants, the general gets." Each time that we had a new commanding general on the base, he would change things around. One example, which I thought was quite humorous, was when we had a general that liked the color brown. Shortly after he took over command of the Army Headquarters, everything on the base that could be painted was changed to brown, including the fire hydrants.

Once I started receiving paychecks, my father asked me to pay him $40 per month for room and board. Having to pay room and board was my first lesson on how to be financially responsible. When I was working, my favorite part of each day was lunchtime. I enjoyed trying to figure out which restaurant to go to next. Toward the end of each workday, my thoughts again turned to food when I called my mother at home and asked her, "What's for dinner tonight, Mom?" Throughout my entire government career, I always took as long as I could for lunch each day. My argument was that it gave me a good break away from my work, which allowed me to return to the office refreshed and able to do more work the rest of the day. It did not take me long to figure out that when you are proficient at what you do, and complete all your work on time, you can sometimes bend the rules a little in your favor.

When I first began working as a secretary, the only way to learn my job was from on-the-job training. Even though I learned almost everything from the senior secretaries, it took me a while to become familiar with the Army lingo and acronyms. Back in the early 70s, the abbreviations used in the Army were not as commonplace in the civilian world. One lesson, which I will never forget, happened one day when I received a phone call while my boss was out of the office. When I told the caller that my boss was not in the office, he said, "Please have him call ASAP!" Assuming that I was supposed to know who he was, he quickly hung up the phone before I could ask him any questions.

My boss was a little confused when he read the phone message I had given him. I had written: "You received a call from Mr. Asap who would like you to call him back right away."

As he stood there laughing at me, he said, "Lisa, there is no Mr. Asap. It is an acronym which stands for 'as soon as possible.' Next time you receive a phone call like this, please ask for a name and a phone number."

After my learning curve from on-the-job training, I became proficient at what I did and won many awards for my work. Most of my awards were for outstanding achievement. But one special award was presented to me by the Inspector General when I performed above and beyond the call of duty during an IG inspection. My father was extremely proud of me when I was presented with that award. My father loved bragging to all his friends about me, telling them how he heard talk from around the Army base that I was the best secretary there. He often said that my typing skills complimented my piano playing and vice versa.

After working as a secretary for over eight years at Fort Meade, I moved to Cape Canaveral, Florida with a job transfer to Patrick Air Force Base. The idea of moving to Florida came about after visiting a good friend of mine who lived in Bradenton, a city located near the Gulf of Mexico between Tampa and St. Petersburg. Her name was Peggy, and we met at the local skating rink in Reisterstown, Maryland. Roller skating was something that I did for over eight years of my life. By hanging out with other skaters, I was able to learn how to skate fairly well, doing dances like the waltz, the tango, and the jitterbug. Another form of skating that I learned was acrobatic skating. I joined a small troupe of women who performed with an older man named Bob Conner. Performing tricks similar to those performed by Olympic ice skaters, he was the only person I ever knew who did them on roller skates.

Whenever we went to the center of the floor to perform our routines, a crowd always gathered and formed a circle around us. Peggy was fascinated with what we did and joined the troupe. My favorite skating trick was the match spin. Using two wooden matches, taped together with masking tape, the trick always drew a huge applause from the crowd. As I glided in a circle around my partner, while he held onto my left hand and skate, he began to spin faster and faster until my other skate left the floor, making me feel as if I were an airplane flying above the wooden skating floor. With the matches tightly clenched between my teeth, he lowered my head close enough to the floor where I could strike the matches—setting them on fire. I then turned my head, protecting my hair from the flames of the match, flying through the air until the flames went out. I finished the trick when my skates safely returned to the floor. Our skating routine was so exciting to watch that we were televised on a weekly show filmed in Baltimore called *PM Magazine*. As a result of growing up in a home with alcohol abuse, I was extremely shy and nervous, and lacked self confidence. One time in elementary school I even flunked a semester in English because I was afraid to speak in front of the class. I was extremely grateful for learning how to do these exhibitions, which helped me to overcome my shyness and gain self confidence.

After my friend Peggy moved to Bradenton, I was absolutely thrilled when she and her boyfriend invited me to visit them for a few days for the Thanksgiving holiday. A strong contrast to the weather we were having in Maryland at the time, the weather when I arrived in Florida was absolutely gorgeous with temperatures in the 80s and clear blue skies. During my visit, I thought it was the coolest thing in the world to walk on the beach during the month of November, breathing in the warm salty air, carefully walking around colorful sea shells in the sand—the entire time realizing it was a freezing 30 degrees back home. I instantly fell in love with Florida, and decided it was where I wanted to live. I had found my paradise—or as my mother used to say—my end of the rainbow. When I returned to Maryland from that vacation, I immediately began working on a job transfer to Florida. It took a lot of persistence and patience. Having no intentions of ever giving up, I searched for every possible job in the state of Florida until I found one. During the cold winter of 1980, I achieved my goal and was transferred from Fort Meade, Maryland, to sunny Patrick Air Force Base, Florida.

When I initially moved to Florida, I moved in temporarily with friends whom I had met on a previous trip. I stayed at their house in Cocoa Beach until I could find a place of my own, and slept in their spare bedroom on a mattress on the floor. A few weeks later, one of their friends found me a small apartment in the city of Cape Canaveral, just north of Cocoa Beach. I thought I had died and gone to Heaven when I first moved to Florida. I spent most of my time on the weekends either going to the beach or going roller skating, occasionally skating on Ocean Beach Boulevard wearing my pink bikini. I felt fortunate to have inherited my mother's athletic abilities, as well as her voluptuous figure. I also inherited her hazel eyes, but at the age of thirteen one of them changed to a different color, giving my eyes a unique look—one eye being hazel and one eye being green. To look at me you would have to stop and think: What is unique about her?

For my new job at Patrick Air Force Base, I worked with the Army Readiness Group—a small office that supported the Army Reserve Centers around the state of Florida. It was commanded by a tough Army colonel who was an expert on the subject of English. Any time one of the secretaries turned in a report with a word spelled incorrectly, they were punished by having to write the word several times on a blackboard in his office. Sometimes he wasn't too nice when he spoke to the secretaries, upsetting me whenever it happened. To fix a bad situation, I decided to have a photo taken of me that would show him who was really in charge at the office. After I showed him the photo, he developed a new attitude toward me and the rest of the secretaries. The photo I had taken was of me sitting in his office chair—smiling—with my feet up on his desk.

For three years I worked for the Army Readiness Group and thoroughly enjoyed my job. Although there were plenty of handsome military men working at the base, I refused to date any of them. I knew that they would eventually be transferred to another Air Force Base, most likely in a colder climate, and I had no intentions of leaving Florida for anyone. Since the state of Florida's population includes a large percentage of tourists and senior citizens, it did not leave me with many choices for single men that were well established in the area. I did date a few guys, but every one of them turned out to be an utter and total disaster. One guy wanted to introduce me to his mother, after our first and only date, and take me with him to live in Minnesota where the winters were unbearable. Then there was the guy who worked with his father in the deep sea fishing business. I spent many hours helping him with his studies to become a captain for the large cruise ships. When he left town for his final exam, I never heard from him again. According to my old neighbors, he did eventually come knocking on my door a few years later, but he was too late. I had already moved out of the apartment. I guess you could say he missed his boat.

Whenever I complained about my boyfriends to my brothers, they always said, "If you ever expect to find a decent man, he'll most likely have to be someone from up north."

During the last few days of visiting with my mother before she died, she made an interesting comment about her thoughts on my love life at the time. Reflecting back on what she said, it was almost as if she was seeing into my future.

"Sweetheart, I don't care for any of the men you've been dating lately and really wish you'd meet someone nice. I know that one day you'll meet someone right for you. And when you do meet that person, everything will go smoothly, without any complications."

Then she added: "And who knows, he may even show up at your front doorstep."

Oddly enough, what she said is exactly what happened, and it was just a few weeks after she died. My neighbors, Mack and Gracie, who lived in the apartment above mine, highly recommended a friend of theirs that they thought I should meet. He was in town for the week, visiting his grandmother who lived in Cocoa Beach. They told me he was a good man, from an excellent family, and he even owned his own business. I met him at my apartment when he rang my doorbell—*standing on my front doorstep*. His name was Donny Jones and he was visiting from Marlboro, Massachusetts. When I answered the door, standing before me was a tall, handsome man—with a look of kindness on his face. He had black hair, brown eyes, and a well-trimmed beard.

Later on in our relationship, he told me: "When you opened your front door and I saw you for the first time, I was certain you weren't the girl my friends told me I'd be meeting, and you must have been her roommate. When I realized who you were, I thought I was a lucky guy to have met someone as beautiful and wonderful as you."

After inviting him into my apartment, we sat on my sofa. I showed him some of my photo albums. And then I made him look through my best cookbooks with me while I pointed out all my favorite recipes. During our conversation, he asked me about going out on a date with him. I hesitated in answering him, thinking about my most recent dating disaster. When I recently stopped dating a man because he would not give up his other girlfriend, he said some pretty mean things to me. When I explained to Donny the mean things that were said to me by my previous boyfriend, he made a comment that touched my heart. After hearing it, I knew this was a man who would never hurt my feelings.

With a kind look on his face, he said, "How can anyone be so mean to someone who is so nice?"

On our first date, he met me for lunch at the Non-Commissioned Officers Club at the base where I worked. I was glad that it was a Thursday because they had honey-dipped fried chicken on the menu that day—very delicious and one of my absolute favorites. While we made our way through the cafeteria line, somehow the subject of having children came up. During the conversation, I told him my mother had six children—which was difficult for her—so I wasn't sure that I really wanted any of my own. He seemed pretty happy and relieved when I told him. Feeling this conversation was something that was usually reserved for much later in a relationship, he provided me with what I thought was a strange elaboration to the conversation.

"Well, I'm glad we got that settled; I don't want any children either."

He called me three times over the next few days to ask me to go out with him. Each time that he called, I turned him down, coming up with a new excuse each time. I even unplugged my phone a few times. Eventually, I made it clear to him how much I loved living in Florida, and had no plans whatsoever of becoming involved with anyone who lived in any of the cold "M" states from up north. The day before he was supposed to go back home, my neighbor Gracie invited me to join her and her husband for dinner. "Lisa, would you be interested in going to dinner with us tonight? We're going to Makatos. It's an excellent Japanese steak house in Melbourne. And by the way, Donny will be joining us if that's OK with you."

Since I had heard good things about the restaurant (especially how good the food was) and I would have two chaperones with me, I decided to go. The old saying, "the way to a man's heart is through his stomach," really should have been written in reference to women as well, especially when it came to me. When Donny arrived to pick us up for dinner, he offered to let my neighbors sit in the front seat and drive the car so that he and I could sit in the back. He was using a car that he borrowed from his brother who lived in St. Petersburg, Florida—a maroon 1974 Barracuda with a white pinstripe painted on the side. Once we arrived at the restaurant and we were seated at our table, the chef arrived with a cart full of food that he would be cooking in front of us. He proceeded to do a few tricks as he started to prepare our meal. After he dropped the salt shaker during one of his tricks, we became a little nervous when he began throwing sharp knives up in the air. After eating our delicious Japanese dinner, and surviving the dinner show, Donny reached for my hand under the table. He continued to hold my hand the entire time until we were back at my apartment.

After that date, he delayed his flight home by a few days so that he could spend more time with me in Florida. When my neighbors told me later on that he delayed his flight home and why, I thought it was really romantic. Since I was an excellent roller skater, I thought I would impress him with my skating abilities, and suggested we go to the local skating rink for our next date. When we arrived at the skating rink, he informed me that he was not a good skater. To help him out, I made sure that his skates were laced up properly.

Before we reached the skating floor, he asked me, "Since I'm not too good at this, could you give me some help?"

"I'll be glad to help you. I've been skating for many years and love teaching other people how to skate."

I thought he was clumsy because the entire time we were skating he kept clinging to me, as if he were a young child hanging on for dear life. He told me later on that he was an excellent skater and just wanted to be close to me. I thought it was sweet of him to say that.

As an added attraction to our date, I demonstrated the match spin for him when my instructor showed up at the skating rink. He just happened to be visiting friends of his in Cocoa Beach and decided to go skating. When I finished the trick, Donny told me he was quite amazed when he watched me, but added that he was concerned about me hurting myself. When he said that to me, I also thought it was a sweet thing for him to say.

On the last day during his visit, we spent the day at Disney World's Magic Kingdom. By this point in time, my senses were telling me that I may not be living in Florida much longer. After he returned to Massachusetts, we wrote letters to each other every day and talked on the telephone every night. Almost every letter that he wrote was tucked inside a Hallmark card with Care Bears on it. A few weeks into our relationship, Donny and his parents, Ted and Lorraine, invited me to visit them in Massachusetts to see the fall foliage. His parents told me that they had a big house with plenty of room for me to stay with them. After I accepted their offer, I flew north to Massachusetts by way of a new airline called *People Express*. Advertised as a no-frills airline, their prices were less expensive than the prices of their competitors. When I made my flight reservation, I was somewhat surprised when they told me not to pay for my flight until after I boarded the aircraft. I was even more surprised by what happened after I boarded the aircraft. Patiently waiting to pay for my flight, I could not believe it when they rolled a cash register down the aisle to collect everyone's money—and that didn't occur until we had reached a safe flying altitude. Whenever I flew with them, I dreaded to think what would happen to any of the passengers if they refused to pay—always looking around the plane to see if there were any parachutes on board.

The plane landed safely—cash register included—and I had my first glimpse of Boston Logan International Airport in Massachusetts. The traffic during the drive from the airport to Marlboro was quite different from what I was used to in Florida. In Cocoa Beach, a bad traffic situation is waiting through more than two red lights to make it through an intersection. In Boston, the traffic was so bad that it seemed like forever before reaching any destination. His parents owned a white three-story house, located on the same property as their family power equipment business. When his father, Ted, opened the business years before, it was originally a bait shop. He started repairing lawnmowers, and with one thing leading to another, he became a full-time power equipment dealer. In the months prior to our meeting, Donny and his younger brother Jimmy had been given the family business to run as their own.

During my visit, we drove up the east coast of New England, all the way to Maine. The scenery was magnificent as we drove through the countryside, taking in the beauty of leaves changing colors, viewing seaside villages, and traveling on roads winding from one lovely town or harbor to the next. He told me he enjoyed showing me the beauty of the landscape where he lived, hoping that I would want to move there one day. Although I enjoyed looking at the landscape, I did not care for the beaches that we stopped at along the way. They were nautical-looking, some of them having lighthouses, but they were a far cry from the pristine beaches I had become accustomed to while living in Florida. On the way home we stopped at a local fish market to buy a few lobsters. His plans were to prepare a traditional lobster dinner for us once we returned to his house in Marlboro.

One evening during my visit, he took me dancing to a nightclub where friends of his played in a band. They were a group of local businessmen who decided to put a band together and play occasionally on weekends. Surprisingly, their music was enjoyable to listen to, and when we danced to their music, it was easy to pick up the beat. Dancing has always been one of my passions in life, most likely inherited from my father. While he was in the service, he had the distinct pleasure of dancing with Ginger Rogers during a special entertainment event for the troops. He bragged about it all the time. When I was a little girl, he used to put my feet on his shoes and dance me around the room, reminiscing by telling me how he used to dance with my mother in their younger days.

That trip was followed by a visit from him to spend the Thanksgiving holiday with me in Florida. When he first arrived, we went to the beach and spent the day swimming in the ocean and walking in the sand to the Cocoa Beach pier. In the evenings, we took romantic walks on the beach under the moonlight. The moon was so bright that it cast a beautiful light that shimmered on the ocean waters as the waves washed ashore. On Thanksgiving Day, I showed off my cooking abilities by preparing him a traditional turkey dinner, similar to the ones that my mother used to make. Thinking back to the Thanksgiving holidays during my childhood, I could still vividly remember what it was like watching my mother cooking in the kitchen. Wearing one of her brightly colored cotton dresses, she stood over the gas stove with her wooden spoon, stirring a mixture of onions and celery, adding spices to the mix, creating an appetizing aroma, making everyone in the house eager for dinner to be served. When I served Thanksgiving dinner this year, Donny really appreciated it.

"Lisa . . . thanks for cooking such a delicious dinner for me. Do you always cook like this?"

"Yes, I do. I love cooking, just like my mother did. By the way, thank you for spending this day with me. It means a lot to me. This is my first Thanksgiving since my mother died."

"I'm so sorry to hear that. It must be difficult for you."

"What makes it even worse is that she had her first heart attack on Thanksgiving Day. It happened while she was in the kitchen fixing our dinner."

"That is so sad. I hope you never have to spend another Thanksgiving alone."

"Thank you Donny. It is sweet of you to say that."

Before he left to go home, we discussed spending the Christmas holidays together up north. A few days after he left, he sent me another Thanksgiving card. When I took the card out of the envelope and read it, I thought it was cute when it said: "Know why I'm passing up the wishbone this Thanksgiving? Cause I already have you in my life! Happy Thanksgiving to someone who's a wish come true." When I opened the card and read the words he had written, my emotions changed to something more serious as I realized the meaning of his message:

Hi Love

I hope you are planning on making it a one-way trip and will be staying with me forever. Because like this card says, you are in my life now and I don't plan on letting you out of it. I love you very much and I miss you.

Love always,

Donny

─────────(**Chapter 4**)─────────

AFTER DISCUSSING WITH DONNY WHAT his true intentions were, I submitted my paperwork to request 90 days leave without pay, giving me sufficient time to search for a government job in Massachusetts. The people I worked with had become like a second family to me, and were hesitant in letting me go. They finally agreed to what I wanted to do, but only if I reassured them that I had plans to be married. When I told Donny I would not be returning to Florida after my next visit, he was thrilled, and quickly arranged a flight to Florida so that he could help me pack my car for the drive up north. With all my personal belongings packed in my blue Plymouth Champ, we drove together to my new home in Marlboro, Massachusetts. When we arrived, his mother and father greeted me with open arms and expressed their happiness that their son had found someone as nice as me. Since there were no immediate jobs available, due to a government hiring freeze, I was concerned about not getting hired before my 90 days expired. As luck would have it, I was hired at Hanscom Air Force Base just one week before my time expired.

Living in Massachusetts was a shock to my system after living in Florida for three years, but it was a nice change having the four seasons again—although I could have gone without having winter. We lived in a two-bedroom ranch that used to belong to his grandmother. When she moved to Florida, she gave him the house as a thank you for all the times that he helped her with house repairs and taking care of her yard—another testament to me that he was a kind man who would never hurt my feelings. The house was walking distance from his parent's house, and the family power equipment business on the same property. After opening the front door to my new home, I entered a small foyer which led into the kitchen and dining room area. Continuing down a short hallway, there were two bedrooms, the bathroom, and the living room. When I looked out the picture window in the living room, I could see a huge maple tree in the front yard. At the back of the house there was another small area with three doors—the first door opened to the garage, the second opened to the backyard, and the third opened to the stairs that went down to the basement. Donny explained to me that he started finishing the basement years ago, but stopped working on it when his first marriage went bad. His first wife was his childhood sweetheart, and he dated her for over eight years before they were married. Although the marriage lasted only six months, it took over five years before he received an annulment from the Catholic Church. I never asked too many questions about her, and just assumed that they were married too young.

The first time that I walked down to the basement, I discovered something that I thought was peculiar. While most of the basement remained unfinished, aside from the washer and dryer hook-ups for the laundry area, he had managed to finish building a small bar with a sink, and there was even a rack with shiny wine glasses hanging from it. I could not figure it out, wondering to myself: Why would finishing a bar be more important than the other projects in the basement that needed to be done? Confused about it, I walked upstairs to ask him why.

"Hi, Sweetie. I saw something in the basement that I'm curious about. With everything that still needs to be done to finish it, why did you build a bar area with a sink? And there are even wine glasses hanging from a rack."

"Well, there was no room to build a bar in the upstairs part of the house, so I had to build it in the basement. A bar always comes in handy when you have company."

"I don't understand. Do your friends drink a lot? I haven't noticed you drinking much since I met you."

"Well, I do have my moments now and then."

Feeling a little uneasy from hearing what he said, I was secretly hoping that I would never see any of those moments, especially after growing up with alcohol during my entire childhood.

The family power equipment business took up most of Donny's time. He spent several hours a day, six days a week, working the business with his younger brother and his parents. I could tell that he was an excellent businessman by the large number of satisfied customers that he had. His company motto was, "After the sale, it's the service that counts." During the spring and summer, he sold and serviced lawnmowers, and during the fall and winter, he did the same for snow blowers. Even though I disliked driving in the snow during the winters, I always enjoyed watching it. Whenever I looked out the living room window, I was fascinated by the unique design of each snowflake, gracefully floating to the ground, gradually changing the landscape to a magical winter wonderland. As a child, I was always thrilled when I woke up on a school day and heard my mother tell me: "You can go back to sleep, Lisa. We had a surprise snowstorm overnight, so school is cancelled for today." Another memory from my childhood is when my father used to take the entire family for a ride in his car after a heavy snowfall. Driving his large green Chrysler Imperial, with my mother in the front seat and the kids in the back seat, he took the car down snow-packed streets throughout the neighborhood, purposely slamming on the brakes, causing the car to spin uncontrollably in the icy snow. As a child I thought these outings were exciting and fun, obviously not realizing at the time how dangerous they were.

Running a power equipment business in Massachusetts was sometimes difficult for my husband. He became fearful at times that we would not have enough money to pay the bills. We had winters when snowstorms were hard to come by, and summer months when it did not rain and the grass dried up. While sitting at our table at the local Ground Round restaurant, on a cold evening in January, I was wondering why my husband was scribbling numbers on a napkin.

"Excuse me, Sweetie. What are you writing on that napkin?"

"I'm just jotting down some numbers, Lisa . . . trying to figure out how to sell some of my snow blowers this week."

"Isn't it supposed to snow tonight? I'm sure you won't have any problems selling them once it snows."

"Have you looked out the window, Lisa? It's pouring down rain outside! It isn't snowing. On the other side of the rain-snow line, only a mile away, they are having a freaking blizzard. That's great for the power equipment dealers in the next town, but it doesn't do me any good at all."

"OK then, I'll make a bet with you. If the rain turns to snow, would you be willing to pay me ten dollars for each inch of snow that we get?"

"Of course I would, but I don't think that's going to happen."

We shook on my bet. Less than a half hour later, as I looked out the windows of the restaurant, I watched as the raindrops changed into heavy wet snowflakes, eventually turning the torrential rainstorm into a snowy blizzard. Two days later, sounding extremely excited, he called me from work.

"This is getting ridiculous! Can we put a cap on that bet of yours and hold it to $250? We have already gotten over 30 inches of snow and it's still coming down like crazy."

Because he spent many hours a day at the power equipment shop, and he knew that I would be lonely, we went shopping in search of a puppy to keep me company. When he first mentioned the idea of finding me a dog, while we were living in Florida, I had visions of having lots of snow when I lived in Massachusetts. I decided that I wanted a dog similar to the sled dogs in Alaska. After visiting a few kennels, we found a beautiful Alaskan malamute puppy with gray and white markings, brown eyes, and a large fluffy tail. We named her Fluffy, but I called her Fluffy Sweetheart most of the time. Even though she grew to be almost 100 pounds, she still acted like a lap dog, sometimes running through the house, jumping over furniture, landing on our laps while we were sitting on the living room sofa. She provided us with great entertainment whenever we had visitors at the house. Our visitors often asked us to open the back door so that Fluffy could come into the house—not realizing that they would end up with a large dog in their laps a few minutes later.

Fluffy loved spending time outdoors and sleeping in her doghouse. She also loved playing in the snow in the wintertime. Her favorite thing was taking walks with us through the neighborhood. The moment we picked up her walking leash, she became so excited that we could hear her tail thumping the floor as she wagged it. We walked her up and down hills through the housing development where we lived, and then took her through the downtown area past the local shops and businesses. If we tried to take a walk without her, and she happened to see us through the chain-link fence in the backyard, she howled like she was in terrible pain until we turned around to take her with us.

Having Fluffy around the house brought a lot of joy into my life. She was the most loyal and loving pet I ever had. She also provided great entertainment on occasion. Whenever we forgot to shut the back door before leaving the house, she enjoyed searching for items in the house to drag outdoors. I could not stop laughing one day when we came home and discovered several pairs of men's underwear and socks scattered all over the backyard—an excellent reminder to the man in the house that he needed to pick up his dirty laundry more often. Fluffy was overly protective of me. If Donny tried to tickle me while Fluffy was in the house, she jumped up on the sofa and tried to bite him. Many times she jumped into the waterbed with us while we were sleeping. If I tried to move my arm after hugging her, she always placed her paw on my arm to keep it there. They say that when you go to Heaven, the pets that you have a love relationship with will be there waiting for you. I know in my heart, when I go to Heaven, Fluffy will be waiting for me with open paws.

Thinking back to the dog that we had while I was growing up, I will never forget what happened to me one Christmas Eve. My sister Gail shared an old tradition with the family where it was once believed that animals could speak on Christmas Eve, right before midnight. Curious about the story and believing it, I stayed up until almost midnight the following Christmas Eve. When I was certain that everyone in the house was sound asleep, I quietly walked down the stairs to visit the family dog, a German shepherd whose name was Trixie. That night I sat on the cold garage floor, wearing my pajamas, and talked to Trixie for several minutes. Patiently waiting for her to speak back to me, I became discouraged and disappointed when she never said a word, realizing then how gullible I was to believe the story in the first place.

Besides walking the dog, another form of exercise that we enjoyed was skiing at our favorite ski resort at Mount Wachusett. Since I had never skied before, Donny was patient with teaching me. He took me on the bunny trail several times until I was able to make it down the hill without falling down. The only part that I disliked was riding up the hill on the ski lift when the cold wind was blowing in my face. Once I did well enough to ski from the top of the mountain, the experience was exhilarating as I made my way through the ski trails, hearing the swooshing sound of the snow beneath me, guiding my skis until I reached the bottom of the mountain. It made me realize why my mother enjoyed skiing as much as she did when she lived in New York. She loved it so much that she went to the ski resorts for the entire weekend. To reach the point of feeling exhilarated when I was skiing, it took several runs down the side of the mountain, falling down many times during each attempt. In order to avoid a catastrophe while I was learning to ski, Donny advised me to turn my skis toward the side of the hill if I felt like I was going too fast. The opportunity presented itself when I suddenly realized I was racing down the hill at an uncontrollable speed. I took his advice and headed for the first hill that I saw. Finding myself airborne as soon as my skis went over the small hill, I somehow managed to land safely on the ground, and continued down the hill at an even faster pace. He quickly came to my rescue and grabbed me before I could crash into anything at the bottom of the hill.

"Lisa! Thank God I was able to catch you before you hurt yourself. Why in the world did you ski over that mogul?"

A little confused, I told him, "But you told me to ski toward the hill on the side if I thought I was going too fast."

"What I meant, Sweetie, was the side of the big hill, not the little mogul. Only the most experienced skiers can handle those. I'm amazed that you were able to land safely without crashing or hurting yourself."

Golfing was another sport that we enjoyed doing together. Whenever the weather cooperated, we went golfing on Sundays at a par-three course in Southborough, Massachusetts. Before I went golfing with Donny, I learned how to play the game by participating in the Air Force sponsored golf tournaments at work. During these tournaments, they had several foursomes on the golf course at one time. To speed things up on the greens, they played the game using a "Shot Gun Scramble" format. The game began with a team of four players at each of the 18 holes on the course. After each player on the team hit his or her golf ball, every ball was picked up except for the one that went the farthest and was still on the fairway. And then everyone hit their next ball from that spot. Since I never played golf before, I was thrilled that they played the game using this format. Otherwise, I would have been hitting my ball all day long just to make it to the putting greens. Once I learned how to play the game fairly well, I began playing with my husband who was a competitive player. He managed to beat my score most of the time, but on one occasion, I had a stroke of good luck and ended the game as the winner. We were at the sixth hole at Stoneybrook Golf Course on a Sunday afternoon. After I hit my ball off the tee, we searched for it to see where it landed. Not finding it anywhere, we gave up looking for it, only to be surprised when we reached the green and discovered that it was in the hole. It was my first and only hole in one.

A few months after moving to Massachusetts, we took a trip to my home in Maryland and Donny was able to meet my father. My father was happy when he met Donny and promised to give us the piano once we were married. During that visit, my dad had a friend staying with him for a few days who was a Catholic priest. Since we had not been to confession for several years, he suggested we do the sacrament of confession right at the house. It felt strange to me when Donny and I took turns confessing our sins to the priest in one of the bedrooms. It was the same bedroom where my mother and father fought all the time while I was growing up. My father was also helpful with making sure that my potential husband had his confirmation papers in order so that we could be married in the Catholic Church. Although I was extremely happy that he was able to meet the new man in my life, I was also saddened that my mother did not have the opportunity to meet him.

Not long after that visit, my father became extremely ill and we lost him to intestinal cancer—only ten short months after losing our mother. When he knew that the end was near, he asked all six children to come home and visit with him for a few days. Initially, he had gone in for surgery to have a blockage removed from his intestines. When they opened him up to operate, they discovered that he was full of cancer and closed him back up without completing the operation. Even though he was feeling excruciating pain, his last wish was to come home for a few days to be with all his children one last time. It was sad when we all went to the house to visit him. We listened to him as he explained how bad the pain was that he was feeling. He also gave us some good advice which I never forgot.

"Kids . . . please take my advice and never take up any of my nasty habits like smoking and drinking. I'm certain that they played a huge role in causing my illness."

The day that my brother Daniel took our father to the hospital for the last time is something that is still vivid in my mind. It was an eerie experience, as if my mother was calling him to be with her. After my brother drove the car up to the hospital entrance, he was greeted by an orderly who asked him if they should bring out a wheelchair for my father. While my brother waited patiently with my father in the car, the orderly went into the hospital to search for the wheelchair. Returning a few minutes later, he pushed the chair over to the car. My father stepped out of the car and carefully stood up with my brother's assistance. After standing up all the way, he looked down at the chair that he was about to sit in. At that moment he began to shake, and his face turned a pale white—as if he had just seen a ghost. My brother glanced over at the chair, wondering what was upsetting my father so much that it caused him to shake. What my brother saw was a name tag still on the chair. It was a name tag that they had forgotten to remove, which belonged to a former patient, a patient who had used the chair many times before—the name tag read, "Amelia."

(Chapter 5)

A FEW MONTHS AFTER MY FATHER died, Donny and I were married in Marlboro, Massachusetts and my name became Mrs. Lisa Jones. We had a beautiful wedding in the local Catholic Church with several of our friends and relatives in attendance. The wedding dress that I wore was borrowed from one of Lorraine's friends. A traditional white satin gown, it had a rosette scoop neckline and beaded lace sleeves. When the priest announced during the ceremony that my parents were there in spirit, I felt a chill go through me as I sensed their presence. It is often said that sometimes women marry their father—or as research and experience shows, they marry a person who has the same qualities they became familiar with while growing up. Although I did not realize it until several years later, marrying my father is exactly what I did. Thinking back to the beginning of our relationship, there were a few clues along the way that I was obviously blind to at the time they happened. To most people these incidents would have been obvious red flags. Because I had grown up with alcohol in the home, and these events were similar to things that I had been used to living with, I looked at them from a different perspective than most people—seeing them as normal. The first clue was a strange phone call I received from my future father-in-law. It was the day before I was scheduled to leave Florida to be with his son in Massachusetts. He seemed like a pretty funny guy when I spoke to him on the phone that day.

"Hi! This is Ted, Donny's father. I want you to know that this is your last chance to decide what you want to do, young lady. Do you want to stay in Florida where it's warm and sunny? Or do you want to move up here to cold Massachusetts and live with this blooming drunken idiot of a son of mine?"

Thinking that he was joking at the time, I politely told him: "You're very funny sir, but I love your son and want to be with him. My mind's already made up that I'm moving to Massachusetts."

The next day I picked Donny up at the airport and drove him to my apartment to help me prepare for the trip up north. After packing everything that I owned into my Plymouth Champ, we hit the road and headed north. Since it was the month of December, the temperature became much colder after we drove a few miles north. As soon as we passed the Georgia line, only three of the four cylinders in my car decided to work. Just like me, my car had become accustomed to the warmer weather, and it was a shock to its system when the temperature dropped. When we reached the New England states, I saw a billboard that reminded me of where I was headed—a large picture of a white Polar Bear, the image still vivid in my mind even to this day.

Making conversation during the drive, I told Donny: "I received a phone call from your father yesterday. While he was talking to me, he made a joke about me moving to Massachusetts to live with you. He asked me if I wanted to stay in Florida or move to Massachusetts, and then jokingly described you as a blooming drunken idiot. Your dad sounds like a real practical joker."

Defending himself, he said, "My father said that! I cannot believe him. He isn't helping me out here very much. Of course I'm not a blooming drunken idiot!"

There were several more hints—a couple of them happening while leading up to and including our wedding reception. For starters, he persuaded me to hold our wedding reception at a drinking establishment—one that I was pretty familiar with from my childhood days.

"Sweetie, I have given it some thought and I think the American Legion is the best place to hold our wedding reception. It's so close to home that all we have to do is walk across the street when the party is over. Isn't that great? We won't have to worry about driving home."

Not realizing he picked the American Legion because their drinks were cheaper than other places, and walking home was a good thing because he may drink too much, I jokingly replied to him, "Well, at least I'll feel right at home since I spent most of my childhood at an American Legion."

Since I wasn't overly excited about where we were holding our wedding reception, I put most of my efforts into making sure everything was perfect at the church. My efforts were rewarded with a beautiful wedding ceremony—which was quite a contrast to the wedding reception that followed. As I waited at the back of the church to walk down the aisle, I admired my future husband standing at the altar. Wearing a black tuxedo and tie, with a silver vest, he looked extremely handsome. The ceremony began with a beautiful version of "Ave Maria," sung by a woman I had personally selected based on her angelic voice. After she sang, and all the guests were seated, the organist began to play *Here Comes the Bride*. Everyone in attendance stood up and turned around to see the beautiful bride at the back of the church. With my younger brother Mark at my side as my escort, I began my slow walk toward the altar. With cameras flashing everywhere, and heads turning to look at me, I was glowing with happiness as I walked toward the man whom I was about to marry. Once we reached the altar and knelt down on the kneeling pad, I could sense that Donny was pretty nervous about the entire event.

Not long after the priest began speaking to the audience, Donny started joking with me. I could not believe it when he said, "Do you think the priest put his deodorant on today? He smells pretty bad."

Once we exchanged our wedding vows and the ceremony was over, we headed down the aisle toward the receiving line. Not really caring for the long ceremony I had chosen, my new husband shared his thoughts with me.

"I don't know why they can't make these things a lot shorter. Then we could get to the party sooner, which is the best part."

When we arrived at the American Legion, the room was nicely decorated with white paper wedding bells hanging from the center of the ceiling, white streamers reaching out to the walls, and pink tablecloths on all the tables. Each table had a centerpiece made from a blue candle holder with blue and white silk flowers around it. The band was set up to the right of the head table and the bar was directly across the room. We were in the building for only a few minutes when I noticed my new husband already had an alcoholic beverage in his hand. Once everyone had a chance to mingle with the other guests, they helped themselves to the food, giving lots of compliments to the chef who prepared it. Even though I did not take part in most of the preparations for the reception, I did arrange for my brother Mark to sing a special song for our first dance—*Always and Forever*, by Heatwave. The first time that I heard the song was during my first visit to see Donny in Massachusetts. It was when he took me dancing to the local club where his friends were playing. After he introduced me to his friends in the band, he whispered something in my ear as they were preparing to play the song.

"I asked my friends to play a special song for us tonight. I want you to know that the words to this song, which they are about to play, will let you know how I feel about you." It was probably the most romantic thing that he ever did for me.

As the reception continued, and we began the usual wedding rituals, I noticed he was drinking more alcohol than he normally did. Thinking that he was just celebrating our happy occasion, I did not think twice about it—at least until everyone gathered around for the ceremonial cutting of the cake. Although cutting the cake is normally a sentimental and romantic moment for the bride and groom, symbolizing the couple's first meal together as husband and wife, an uneasy feeling came over me as we sliced the first piece of cake together. When he began to feed it to me, the younger relatives on his side of the family began cheering for him, becoming louder and louder, until he deliberately smashed the piece of cake into my face. Standing there humiliated, ignoring his relatives who were cheering for me to do the same thing, I gently fed him his piece of cake to complete the ceremony. My sister Gail told me later in the evening that she was concerned about me, and thought he may have a mean streak in him. I reassured her that he was a kind and loving man, and had been extremely nice to me during the time that I knew him before our wedding.

The next incident occurred when we drove to the picturesque Grist Mill at the Wayside Inn in Sudbury. A popular location for weddings, the Grist Mill presented a striking background for wedding photos. Since the gate was not open when we arrived, my new husband decided to jump over it. He then grabbed me and threw me over his shoulder, with my wedding gown still on, and then jokingly told me that he was carrying me over the threshold. The wedding photographer even took a picture of it. Needless to say, with everything that happened on that day, our honeymoon night was not exactly something you would read about in a typical romance novel. If these things did not tip me off, I should have realized something was wrong when I noticed he was holding a beer bottle in his hand in one of our wedding photos.

To his credit, he did manage to keep his drinking under control for many years during our marriage and we were extremely happy together. We were considered the perfect couple by our friends, who even nicknamed us Barbie and Ken. Every day he called me at work, just to tell me that he loved me. He was the most loyal and loving husband that anyone could ever ask for. We did everything together—played golf, went dancing, took walks, went to the movies, and occasionally went to the shopping mall. Early on in our marriage, we established every Friday night as date night. Many times on Friday night, we had dinner with his cousin Carol at the Ground Round restaurant in Worcester. Even though the restaurant was known for serving whole peanuts to their customers, and not discouraging them from throwing shells on the floor, I much preferred their popcorn with the cheese salt flavoring. After dinner, we drove to Carol's house and visited with her and her mother, Violet. I dearly loved his Aunt

Violet and Cousin Carol and enjoyed every moment that we spent with them.

Since I was an orphan, recently losing my mother and father, it was comforting to know that I had a family again. I loved his parents and they loved me. They treated me as if I were the daughter they never had. Not long after we were married, his parents moved to Cocoa Beach, Florida, to live in their house on the beach. Thinking about the day when we would move to Florida, and where we would live, I made a suggestion to my new husband.

"Sweetie, if we wait ten years from now to buy a house in Florida, we may not be able to afford one. Why don't we ask your parents to see if they can find a house for us now? We can make the down payment with the money I inherited from my father, and we can rent it out which will pay for most of the mortgage each month."

"That's a great idea, Lisa. I'll ask them to try and find one on the water. I would love to have a dock in our backyard for a fishing boat."

Within a few weeks, his parents found a house on the water and we purchased our first piece of real estate together. It was located at the end of a deep-water canal which led into the Banana River. Over the next few years, the power equipment business did extremely well, which allowed us to purchase additional rental properties in Cocoa Beach. We were thankful that his parents were able to manage our property until we were able to move to Florida. Since they were retired, it was a good thing for them because it gave them something to keep them busy. The second house that we purchased was the same house that I lived in when I first moved to Florida. It was the house where I slept on a mattress that was on the floor. I had no clue at the time that my future in-laws—whose son I would meet three years later—just bought a house right around the corner the month before.

My husband told me many times that I was his inspiration and the reason why the family business did as well as it did. When larger stores began carrying the same brands as the small power equipment businesses, it made it difficult for them to compete and stay in business. It became so bad that it caused some of Donny's competitors to go out of business. To give his business a competitive edge, he had to be creative with his marketing strategies. Focusing more on the service end of the business, he designed a program where he picked up his customers' lawnmowers at the end of the mowing season, stored them during the winter, and then serviced them in the spring before returning them to his customers. He did the same thing with snow blowers when he picked them up at the end of the snow season and returned them in the fall.

Since his parents had a place for us to stay in Florida, we were able to visit several times a year. During many of our visits, we took vacations on the cruise ships out of Port Canaveral. We looked so happy and content during these cruises that the other passengers often asked us if we were newlyweds. We always gave them the same answer. "No, we're not newlyweds. We have no children." On more than a few occasions, Donny made it perfectly clear to me that he did not want children. I wasn't too surprised since he brought it up the first week that I met him. He always told me he was afraid he would be too worried about them, and often times jokingly added that he wanted to have all the toys.

He also joked about it when we went to restaurants to eat. Whenever he heard a baby screaming at a nearby table, he would look at me and say, "Thank you, Dear."

To his credit, he also told me that we would talk about it if I ever decided that I really wanted them. Sadly enough, a few years after we were married, my ability to have children was taken away from me. I developed large tumors on my uterus, which had to be removed by a partial hysterectomy. Every time that I went to a baby shower, or saw someone with a newborn baby, I felt great sadness knowing that I could never have any of my own. The only good thing about not having children was that it made things easier for us financially. Growing up with five brothers and sisters, I remember many times hearing my mother and father complaining about how much money it cost to raise children.

Since my father had promised me the piano after I married Donny, we knew that we eventually had to take a trip to Maryland to pick it up. The time came for us to do that when my sister Gail told us she needed to remove everything from my father's house. I thought it was amazing when she told me she had a buyer for the house before she even had a chance to put it on the market. I made arrangements with my three brothers to meet us at the house when we arrived in Maryland to pick up the piano. After driving for over seven hours in Donny's silver Nissan pick-up truck, we pulled into the driveway to load up the piano. Expecting my brothers to show up with everything that we needed to load the piano into the back of the truck, we did not bring any rope or dollies with us. As luck would have it, none of my brothers could make it that day. While we were trying to figure out what to do, something magical happened. Knowing that my father wanted me to have the piano, I believe that he had something to do with what happened next. When the doorbell rang and I opened the front door, I saw two husky-looking men standing on the front doorstep.

"Hi. Can I help you gentlemen?"

"Yes you can. We're here to pick up the dresser that we're going to buy from someone named Gail."

I let them into the house and told my sister that they had arrived. After they paid for the dresser and I watched how easily they loaded it into their truck, I had to ask them, "What do you two fellows do for a living?"

I was amazed when they said, "We're piano movers."

I immediately replied, "Oh boy! Do I have a job for you!"

They were very kind and helpful and did everything that was required to safely load my piano into the back of the pick-up truck. When they were finished, I looked up and said, "Thanks, Dad."

While we lived in Massachusetts, I had the opportunity to work with two different programs with the Air Force at Hanscom Air Force Base. The first job that I had was working in the AWACS (Airborne Warning and Control Systems) Program Office. During this time I had the rare opportunity to work with a woman who was destined to do great things with the Air Force. She was an Air Force major at the time and her name was Leslie Kenne. She was by far the best boss I ever had. A bundle of energy, she kept everyone in the office motivated at all times. Each morning she started the day with her usual, "Are we having fun yet?" I learned an important lesson from her one day when she asked me a question that I did not have the answer to. When I responded with the usual, "I do not know," she gave me a response that I have never forgotten.

"Lisa . . . when someone says something to you that you don't know the answer to, never tell them that you do not know. The more professional response is always telling them that you do not know the answer but are willing to find out for them."

After working with her for only a few days, I felt extremely honored when she told me that I was the best secretary she ever had. Working for her was so rewarding that I did not apply for other jobs, even though a few did become available to me during the time that I worked for her. She was pleased that I enjoyed working with her, and told me I could apply for all the jobs I wanted after she moved on to her next assignment. Eventually she did move on, and had an extraordinary career with the Air Force. Several years later she reached the rank of three-star general.

For my next position, I worked as an executive secretary for an Air Force colonel who was the director of the AWACS program. Although he was a great boss, he became verbally abusive at times with his employees. Whenever he became upset with something, he raised his voice and yelled at whoever was near him at the time. When I happened to be that person and he took his anger out on me, I drove him crazy when I just stood there and smiled at him. It was something that I learned to do while growing up with anger in the home. Working in the front office required a lot of patience on my part, having to deal with many unique personalities throughout the day. My boss repeatedly told other people in the office that I was like the eye of the hurricane—always remaining calm—even though everything around me was in total chaos.

After working with that program for a few years, I transferred my job to the Joint Surveillance Target Attack Radar System (Joint STARS) program office. The program was only a few years old at the time. During the time that I worked with them, they were still in the testing phase. Their testing site, which included two test aircraft, was located at an airport in Melbourne, Florida. We were told that if the program survived until they went into full production, the system would play a vital role with American forces in combat situations. I thought the coolest part about the aircraft was its ability to fly in safe American airspace and look deep behind enemy lines with its forward-looking radar. The aircraft then transmitted information to the ground troops—letting them know if they were heading into enemy troops or tanks. Even though it was the most advanced targeting and battle management system in the world, military budgets were being cut at the time, and it was not certain if the program would survive long enough to go into full production.

When Kuwait was invaded during Desert Storm in August of 1990, my husband came up with a brilliant idea. With a proud look on his face, he said, "Why don't you talk to your boss tomorrow morning and recommend that they send their two test aircraft to Kuwait. Maybe they can help out with the war efforts if they do."

Agreeing that it was a great idea, the next day I approached the colonel in charge of the program.

"Sir, my husband has an idea that I would like to share with you. He feels that we could help out with the war efforts if we were to send our two test aircraft over to Kuwait."

"That is an excellent idea, Lisa. But the only problem is I'm not sure if the airplanes will work properly. They are still going through their testing phase."

I quickly responded, "Well, they are trying to shut the program down. What do we have to lose?"

A week after that discussion, my boss made a huge announcement at work. The two airplanes were being deployed to Kuwait. When I asked him whose idea it was, he told me that an Army general came up with the idea. Even though I did not receive credit for my husband's suggestion, I still felt good that it happened. The deployment was a huge success—and saved the lives of many soldiers who were fighting on the ground. It was the most rewarding experience I ever had while serving as a secretary with the military. The success of the two aircraft in Desert Storm also resulted in the program being saved—going into full production.

The most fun that I ever had while working with the Air Force was when I had the pleasure of attending an event called "The Air Force Dining Out"—a formal military tradition where the Air Force officers wore their dress blues and the civilians wore formal attire, as if they were attending a fancy ball. I always enjoyed dressing up for these events. The funniest part was something referred to as "The Mess," which had over 20 rules they had to abide by during the formal part of the evening. The one rule that I remember as being the funniest was, "Thou shalt not leave the mess whilst convened; military protocol overrides all calls of nature." If any of the rules of the mess were ever broken, the person breaking the rule had to go to the grog bowl—a gross concoction consisting of strange liquid ingredients. Once at the grog bowl, they had to fill their cup, drink it without removing it from their lips, and then place it upside down on top of their head. There were also a couple of military salutes included in this routine. While it was definitely fun to watch, I was thankful that I never had to go to the grog bowl myself.

Donny and I had our first argument during one of these events. Since his father was a high-ranking enlisted man in the Air Force, Donny shared his opinion that officers did not do any of the work because the enlisted troops did it all. I became angry with him when he had too much to drink and then decided to talk to the Commanding General. Expressing his opinion with the general, he said, "You know what? I really wish I would have joined the Air Force as an officer, instead of running my own business. I'm really tired of having to work so hard for a living." Having a lot more insight into my relationship with my husband than I did, after this incident occurred, the general began suggesting to me that I try for a higher paying position—just in case I ever decide to divorce my husband.

Every winter when I missed the warm weather, Donny reminded me of the promise he made when I first moved to Massachusetts. "Sweetie, ten years from now, I promise we'll move back to Florida."

After living in Massachusetts for a few years, I found myself becoming depressed during the cold and dreary days of winter. My personality was not as bubbly as it was during the spring, summer, and fall. With a lot of persistence and an enormous amount of prayer, I finally made his promise come true—almost exactly ten years after we met. To achieve this miraculous event, I called the job hotline at Patrick Air Force Base religiously every day to see what job openings were available. I prayed intensely—several times a day—and do not remember ever praying as hard for anything during my entire life. The odds of being hired for any job that was offered were slim to none because the government had what was called a stopper list. Whenever a secretarial job became available, it was offered only to military spouses who needed a job, or to government employees who had lost their jobs. If no one from those two categories needed a job at the time that it was advertised, then the position became available to everyone in the government who qualified and applied for it.

In addition to praying diligently every day, I spent many hours perfecting my job resume, adding letters of recommendation from colonels and generals whom I had worked with over the years. Once I mailed my resume to the civilian personnel office, I called them and asked for confirmation that they received it. I was told that they could not give me confirmation right away because there were too many resumes on file to look through. To be certain that I did not miss out on any opportunities, in case my resume got lost in the mail, I immediately sent them another copy using overnight express mail—forcing them to send me a signed receipt when it arrived.

Continuing to call the job hotline every day, I became extremely excited when they announced a permanent secretarial position at Cape Canaveral Air Force Station. It was only a few miles from where Donny's parents lived in Cocoa Beach. From the first moment that I heard the job announcement over the phone, I knew with great certainty that the job was mine. It was a distinct feeling of knowing—a feeling that I believe comes from another sense, one that we are not always in touch with. When I called the personnel office for additional information on the position, I learned that 40 out of the over 200 resumes that qualified were being delivered to the hiring official the next day. Also learning where the position was, I immediately tracked down the office that was doing the hiring and gave them a call to tell them what my intentions were.

"Hello, this is Lisa Jones. I live in Massachusetts and have applied for a job in your office. According to the civilian personnel office, they received over 200 applications for the secretarial position you have available. They also told me that those 200 applications have been narrowed down to 40, and they will be put on your desk tomorrow morning."

I took a few breaths and continued to speak. "I want you to know that you may as well throw them all away except for mine. No one else is better qualified for that job than I am. And I am positive that no one else wants that job as much as I do."

The man on the phone was somewhat surprised by what I said, and told me that although I sounded positive about my qualifications, my application would be reviewed along with all the others.

Then I added: "Oh, by the way. If you decide to hire me, I will still be able to report for duty two weeks after I'm hired, even though I live over thirteen hundred miles away in New England. I already have a place to live with my in-laws and everything I need is already packed."

A few days later, I received a phone call from my new boss telling me that I had been selected for the position. He told me that his deputy had reviewed all the resumes, and put mine in the top three based on my qualifications and letters of recommendation—and did so without any knowledge of the phone call that I had made. At that moment, I felt as if a giant weight had been lifted from my shoulders. I was going back to Florida! Filled with excitement and enthusiasm, I was eager to tell everyone my good news. Within a matter of minutes, pretty much everyone in the entire building knew that I was moving to Florida. Everyone who heard the news was absolutely amazed—

convinced before that it was an impossible goal which I would never be able to achieve. Ted and Lorraine were almost in shock when they heard the news. They had to turn away a tenant to whom they had just rented the mother-in-law apartment. When I shared the news with my husband, he was more shocked about it than anyone. Although he was happy for me that I found a job in Florida, he was not ready to leave the family business.

"That's fantastic news, Lisa, and I know how happy you must be. You're probably the most optimistic and persistent person I've ever known, and it certainly paid off for you. The only problem is I won't be ready to be with you full-time for another year or two. I have to make sure that the business will survive without me being here."

(Chapter 6)

O VER THE NEXT TWO WEEKS, we packed all my personal belongings into my silver Toyota Celica, and then began the 21-hour drive to Cocoa Beach, Florida. Once we drove onto the main highway, Donny inserted a cassette tape into the tape player. Before he pushed the button to play what was on the tape, he said, "Since I won't be with you all the time, I made a special tape for you. I recorded all your favorite songs. And in between each song I recorded my voice so you can hear me telling you how much I love you and I miss you."

"Thank you, Sweetie. That's so romantic that you did that."

Listening to everything that he recorded, I had mixed emotions as I thought about how wonderful it was that we were moving to Florida, but also how sad it was that he would not be with me all the time.

We were fortunate that the house his parents owned had a mother-in-law apartment that I could move into. It was a nice place to live, and it took me only 12 minutes to drive to work. Shortly after moving in, I very appropriately renamed it the "daughter-in-law apartment." I was in Heaven again having the beach right across the street. The apartment had a small living room with a view of the beach when I looked out the window, a tiny kitchen with barely enough room for a table, and one bedroom with a tiny bathroom and a closet. Even though there wasn't much room in the apartment, I thought of all the positive things about living there. Cleaning it would be easy, I could decorate it any way that I chose to, the ocean and beach were right across the street, and Ted and Lorraine lived right next door where I could visit them at any time.

My new job was with the 45th Space Wing at Cape Canaveral Air Force Station. It was the most exciting job I ever had. My office was in a large, double-wide trailer, located close to the two launch pads for the Delta II rockets. Because my desk was next to the snack area, I had the opportunity to chat with everyone who came into the trailer wanting to buy refreshments. When my new boss gave me the usual safety briefing that is given to new employees, something he said took me by surprise, and was a little out of the ordinary for these types of briefings. When he began my briefing, he informed me that I should be aware of the usual safety hazards in the office—paper cuts when opening the mail, tripping hazards like extension cords under the carpet, and filing cabinets falling over and injuring me if I open all the drawers at the same time.

Then he added something quite unusual when he said, "Oh, by the way. I forgot one thing. The day before launch—when we fuel the rocket—there's a chance that the rocket could blow up."

After hearing that, I made a point of always calling in sick on the days when they fueled the rocket. On the days before they fueled the rocket, I took home any valuables that I had at work, which kept them safe should anything go wrong with the launch. Other employees gave me a hard time when I took stuff home with me, but I thought it was just good common sense. After working there for about two years, I was reassigned to a new job with the Safety Office at Patrick Air Force Base. Within a few weeks after I was reassigned to my new position, there was an anomaly at the launch complex on January 17, 1997. A Delta II rocket exploded—only thirteen seconds after lift-off—and destroyed everything in the trailers near the launch pad. Luckily, the employees who worked in the trailers did not work there on launch days for obvious safety reasons. However, the eighty people who worked in the blockhouse—located right next to the launch pad—had a pretty scary experience that day.

After the anomaly, some of the people who were working inside the blockhouse told me what it was like when the rocket exploded and rocket debris began falling from the sky. When large pieces of rocket debris landed on the roof of the blockhouse, they said it sounded as if a giant was stepping on it. They also heard explosions coming from the parking lot, as well as the sound of tires popping on cars as they were melting from the heat of the explosion. It became even scarier for them when smoke started coming into the blockhouse. Fortunately, no one was injured in the event—solely because of the efforts of the 45th Space Wing Safety Office—who insisted that they reinforce the walls and the roof of the blockhouse years before. Needless to say, eighty people vowed to never work in the blockhouse again and launch operations were moved to a new location farther away from the launch pads.

While I worked at the Delta launch complex, I had the opportunity to work as an extra for a television series being filmed in one of the aircraft hangars. The storyline, based around the lives of shuttle astronauts, was called *The Cape*. The star of the show was Corbin Bernsen. He is a famous actor who blazed to TV stardom in 1986 as divorce lawyer Arnie Becker in the TV series "L.A. Law." Since I was not a big fan of the show he starred in, I did not know who he was—that is until I met him accidentally during the first day of filming. Once I arrived at the aircraft hangar, I was told to sit in a room with the other extras. We were given strict instructions not to leave the area; and when they were ready to film the part we had been selected for, they would let us know. Becoming bored very quickly and also curious about the film industry, I decided to take a stroll through the building to see what was going on. Discovering a cool looking director's chair, I decided to sit in it and imagined that I was one of the stars in the show.

A few minutes later, a rugged, good looking man approached me and said, "It's OK to sit there if you want. I'll just trade chairs with you because I don't like that chair anyway."

Immediately, I apologized and said, "Who are you? Are you the star of the show or something?"

"Yes I am, sort of. My name is Corbin Bernsen."

I told him who I was and asked him how to spell his name, confessing that I had not heard of him before. We had a nice conversation where I learned that he lived in England with his gorgeous wife, who was also a film star, and they had a beautiful set of twins. He was excited about his wife visiting him in Florida the following week. Once I discovered that he was a famous actor, starring in a television show which I had never watched, I became excited about working with him.

For my scene, I played the part of a NASA engineer working in the hangar during a space shuttle launch. My part was to act like I was talking on the phone, and then walk toward Corbin as he passed by me, from the opposite direction, to handle an emergency situation. When I asked the director what I was supposed to be saying on the phone, he screamed at me.

"You are not supposed to say anything! If you do, we'll get into big trouble with the Actors Guild."

Apparently, once an extra says even a single word during filming, they automatically become a member of the Actors Guild and have to be paid much higher wages. The scene that I was in had to be shot several times before the director was happy with it. During one of the takes, I almost tripped Corbin when he walked by me, thinking it was pretty funny when it happened. After working with him on the set for several days, I was not at all surprised when he recognized me in public one day. We ran into him when Donny and I went to the Yen Yen Chinese restaurant in Cocoa Beach with our friends Jim and Sonja. In addition to being known for their delicious Chinese gourmet food, they were also known for their occasional famous guests who chose to dine there, especially during the time when *The Cape* series was being filmed in the local area. As we strolled through the restaurant toward our table, we passed a booth where Corbin was having dinner with two other people. I was thrilled when he recognized me and even interrupted his conversation with his friends to say hello. It gave me the opportunity to introduce him to my husband and the couple who were dining with us. All in all, being an extra for a television series was an exciting experience for me, and it was even more exciting when I saw myself on television.

Working at the Cape presented me with another opportunity to play the part of an extra a few years later. I played a small part in a feature movie with Jodi Foster called *Contact*. I was chosen, along with 2,500 other people, to be part of a crowd watching the spacecraft during the launch countdown. Oddly enough, each person was given a dress code for the scene and I was instructed to wear green socks. Not having much time to look for them, the only pair of green socks that I could find had a bright neon color. Minutes before filming began; employees from the film crew walked through the crowd to check things out. I could not believe it when they told me to remove my green socks because they were too bright for the cameras.

I told them, "You must be crazy! I am part of a crowd of over 2,500 people. Who is going to even see the color of my socks?"

"We're sorry, miss, but we think they're just too bright for the cameras."

Losing my argument, still trying to figure out what they were thinking (since the cameras were mounted on a helicopter flying overhead), I reluctantly took off my green socks.

I was instructed, along with everyone else, not to look up at the helicopters while they were flying over the crowd. They said it would ruin the scene if anyone looked up while the cameras were filming—the reason being that we were supposed to be looking at the spacecraft, not up in the air. For my part, I was given a souvenir paddle that I had to wave with enthusiasm while jumping up and down, doing it all during the launch countdown for the spacecraft. Before they began filming, I noticed a camera mounted on scaffolding not far away from where I was standing. Being the ham that I am, I smiled at the camera while I was jumping up and down and waving my paddle. After they finished filming, I told all my friends about my big scene, hoping they would be able to see me in the crowd when the movie came out. Months later, when the movie was released to local theaters, I received a phone call from my sister Gail.

"Hi, Lisa. I just got back from seeing the movie *Contact* and was excited when I saw you. You were jumping up and down in the scene where you told me to look for you—and I could see you, right up there on the big screen!"

Thrilled that she was able to see me, I responded with an astounding "Wow!"

On the work side of things, my job at Cape Canaveral was rewarding and exciting as I was able to watch the assembly of every Delta rocket before they launched it into space. My commute to work took me along the ocean, with a spectacular view of the cruise ships at the port. On the way home, I enjoyed waving at the passengers on the ships as they were preparing to head out to sea.

Living in Florida again gave me a wonderful feeling. The only thing missing was my husband—who spent more time in Massachusetts with his power equipment business than he spent with me in Florida. I understood that he had a business to run, but it still bothered me that he could not find a way to be with me full-time. After all, for many years we talked about the two of us going back to Florida together and how wonderful it would be. Being with him for a few weeks, and then being without him for a month or more, was an emotional roller coaster—leaving me feeling sad when he left, happy when he came back, and then sad again when he left. What made it even more difficult for me was listening to friends and co-workers who constantly commented on the situation. They told me that if he really loved me, there was no way that he could stay away from me for as long as he did. When I told him this, he reminded me of his commitment to the business, and promised me that it would not be much longer.

After living with Donny's parents for over a year and a half, we finally left the daughter-in-law apartment and moved into our own home. Every vision we had shared together was about to become a reality—remodeling our home to make it our dream house, taking boat rides from our own dock, and sharing our new home with friends and family. As we walked into the house that was now ours to live in, we looked past the empty living room and focused on the view of the canal through the picture window. Part of the Intercoastal Waterway, the canal in our backyard flowed into the Banana River, just a few minutes by boat to the navigational locks—our gateway into the port and the Atlantic Ocean. Since we were only a few blocks away from the beach, we took many walks there in the evenings when it was cool. Our journey normally took us through the streets in our neighborhood, over to the world famous Ron Jon's Surf Shop, continuing to the beach, and eventually heading back to the house with our shoes full of sand. During these walks, we discussed everything from remodeling the house to the vacations that we would be taking.

Over the next few years, we added a huge addition to the house, doubled the size of the kitchen, changed the back porch to a Florida room, and added an in-ground swimming pool to the backyard. Once that work was completed by contractors, Donny did a large amount of the finish work himself. Being quite the handyman—and a perfectionist with everything that he did—he spent many long hours turning our home into a beautiful place to live. Although he completed several projects, doing a wonderful job with each of them, there were a few projects that remained undone—just like the basement in our home in Massachusetts.

Whenever our friends asked us when the house renovations would be complete, he always gave them the same answer and said, "If I finish the house, I'm afraid something might happen to me, and then some other man will enjoy living here." I could never understand why he would say such a thing.

In between our many construction projects, we took vacations, taking advantage of the availability of cruise ships at nearby Port Canaveral. Our favorite ship was Premier Cruise Line's *Majestic*, the only one small enough to cruise to the Abaco Islands and make its way into the smaller inlets. The best part of the cruise was when the ship anchored off Great Guana Cay for two days. Using tenders (a nautical term for small boats), we were shuttled back and forth to the island's beaches where we had many activities to choose from—sailing, windsurfing, parasailing, snorkeling, jet skiing, and kayaking. Our favorite activity was snorkeling, where we enjoyed swimming through the island's rich, shallow reefs, and interacting with the brightly colored fish. Even though the fish were advertised as being friendly, my husband encountered some rather unfriendly fish—such as moray eels and barracudas—when he swam with the advanced snorkeling group into deeper waters. He was thrilled when he showed me the photos that he took with our underwater camera. In the evening, we attended a spectacular variety show on the island at an outdoor theater. The show consisted of singers and dancers, sometimes using fire, which was pretty fascinating to watch at night. After the show we enjoyed relaxing in one of the many hammocks on the island, looking up through the coconut palms at the moon and the stars, glancing at our ship anchored off shore, wondering if we should go back to the ship, or if we should just stay on the island all night and sleep in the hammock.

Whenever our cruises came to an end, we felt sorry for the other passengers who had to return home to cold and snowy climates. Feeling like we were still on vacation when we came home, it made us appreciate where we lived. One of the things that Donny appreciated most about living in Cocoa Beach was surf fishing for bluefish from the beach. Often joined by his father, Ted, and his older brother, Bobby, the three of them usually fished early in the morning. A lot taller than Donny, his brother Bobby had long brown hair which he often wore in a pony tail. After he retired from the Air Force, he found a job with the US Post Office, which is where he met his lovely wife Donna. He was a loving father of three girls and several grandchildren from his first marriage. Many times Bobby brought Donna with him when he took our small boat into the river to go fishing. Occasionally, he took the boat into the ocean if the waters were calm enough. A blue and white 17-foot Thunderbird outboard, the boat was powered by a 90 horsepower Yamaha motor. When our boat was not being used for fishing, Donny and I enjoyed navigating it through the canals and into the open river. Once we made it past the channel markers, he pulled on the throttle and took it up to full speed. The ride was an exhilarating experience, which gave us the distinct feeling that we were riding on a cushion of air. As he proudly stood behind the wheel, I sat at the bow of the boat, feeling the salt spray in my face and the wind dancing through my hair. When I turned my head to look at him, I could tell by the look in his eyes that he was happy—and we would say in unison, "This is the life!"

His biggest dream, which he talked about often, was to put our house on the rental market so that we could live on a large catamaran. The master plan included docking the boat behind the house, and then sailing it to the Caribbean islands to do island hopping. He thought about adding a motor to the back of the catamaran to give us power when the winds were not strong enough to sail. Even though it was just a dream of his, it was something that might be possible once I retired from my government job.

Occasionally, we took vacations with our friends Jim and Sonja to exotic locations like Puerto Vallarta, Mexico. Located on Mexico's Pacific coast, the town was originally a small fishing village with a population of about 10,000. In 1964, the town became world famous when Elizabeth Taylor and Richard Burton stayed there during the filming of *Night of the Iguana*. The first time that we vacationed there with Jim and Sonja was when we lived up north. We had to fly from Massachusetts to Dallas, where we met them before continuing to Mexico. As we drove on the Massachusetts Turnpike on that cold, snowy morning in the month of January, we were anxious about making it to the airport on time. With a snowstorm moving into the area, we were also concerned that our flight may even be cancelled. Thrilled when we arrived on time, and the flight was not cancelled, we were happy to board the aircraft. After waiting for several minutes while they de-iced the aircraft, we finally headed down the runway to take off. After the plane left the runway and climbed into the sky, we felt a sigh of relief as we looked down at the ground below us, completely covered with a white blanket of snow. The flight from Dallas to Mexico was a much smoother operation.

When we arrived at our final destination in Puerto Vallarta, the weather was absolutely gorgeous, a strong contrast to the weather earlier that day in Massachusetts. We were greeted by our host who drove us to the hotel where we would spend the next ten days—a luxury resort located on the Mexican Riviera, with a magnificent view of the Pacific Ocean. Although the resort was exquisite—with all the modern facilities available to man—other areas that we visited were not quite as nice. There was the supermarket where refrigeration was so limited that they had to keep everything on ice that was perishable, not to mention the many bathrooms which had no plumbing or running water. Visiting places like Mexico always gave me a greater appreciation for the luxuries that we have at home which we often take for granted.

In addition to having good friends to go on vacation with like Jim and Sonja, they were nice to have around when my husband was working in Massachusetts. I met Sonja when she was the secretary for the commander of the Joint STARS test facility in Melbourne, Florida. We came to know each other by talking on the phone every day, coordinating meetings and trips for our bosses. An intelligent woman with short blonde hair, she was one of the best secretaries I ever had the pleasure of working with. I loved listening to her many lovely stories from when she lived in Lexington, Kentucky.

During one of the months that my husband was away, she invited me to accompany her and her husband Jim to an Air Force Dining Out—just like the ones I attended when I lived in Massachusetts. Making myself look beautiful, like I always did for these events, I wore a green sequin dress. When we arrived at the Officers Club, we joined the cocktail party which was already in progress. We had about twenty minutes to socialize before the formal part of the evening began. Thinking that I looked really good in my new dress, I decided to have my picture taken so that I could send it to my husband. Looking around the club for the best spot to take the picture, I noticed a shiny black baby grand piano, thinking how cool it would be to pose for my picture while sitting on top of it. I gave my camera to my friends, and then attempted to hoist myself onto the top of the piano. Not being successful, I looked around for someone to help me and noticed a tall military man standing close by. Since he was wearing one of the new military uniforms, it wasn't obvious what his rank was.

I approached him and asked for help. "Sir . . . would you mind helping me get up on top of this piano so I can have my picture taken?"

"Not at all. I would be happy to help you out."

While he grabbed my waist, I pushed myself up with my arms, and then positioned myself to where I could sit on the piano comfortably. Sitting up there feeling proud, I posed while my friends took a few pictures of me. I even posed for a photo with the gentleman who assisted me.

Once he helped me off the piano, I smiled at him as I said, "Thank you very much, sir, for helping me out. By the way, my name is Lisa. What is your name?"

Smiling at me, he said, "My name is General Adams. I am the guest speaker for this evening." I was so embarrassed that I did not know what to say. In addition to being totally embarrassed, I managed to have a good time that night—dancing with my friends, eating a delicious dinner, and of course watching the rituals of "The Mess" with the infamous grog bowl.

Knowing that I had a passion for dancing, Donny suggested we take ballroom dance classes, as long as they could be scheduled during the times when he was in Florida. We first went to a local dance club to try a few introductory classes. After taking four inexpensive lessons in ballroom dance, our instructors talked us into a more serious commitment and we scheduled several more. They were fairly expensive, costing thousands of dollars annually, but he still signed up for them. His reasoning was that he wanted me to be happy. It was a wonderful experience for me, especially when we attended the social dances with the other students on the weekends. The older women at these events often fought over the male instructors for dances. I could understand why because I felt like Cinderella every time they waltzed me around the dance floor. The older women also liked dancing with my husband, but commented a few times that his timing was off. Knowing he had a few drinks before the event, I gave them a little smirk and said, "I believe he's on Miller time tonight." At the end of our first year of lessons, we had to renegotiate our contract with the dance club. They brought us into a tiny room where we sat down to discuss the details.

"Okay, Donny and Lisa. Now that you've learned a few dances, where would you like to go from here?"

After telling them all the dances that we would like to learn over the next year, they put some figures together that were quite surprising.

"Well … if you want to learn all the dances you just mentioned, you're going to need more lessons than you did last year. We estimate the cost for those lessons to be around $10,000. Are we in the ballpark here with these figures?"

Looking at the instructor as if he was off his rocker, my husband immediately said, "Are you crazy? We are not even on the same planet with those figures!"

After significantly reducing the number of lessons we would take, we agreed on a more reasonable price and continued for another year.

Another form of dancing that I came to love was belly dancing. When my girlfriends Lenora and Erin suggested we do something new for exercise, we signed up for belly dancing classes from a local instructor named Delbar. It was one of the best things I ever did while living in Florida. Opening up a whole new world for me, it gave me the opportunity to make several good friends during the process of learning the dance. The class was taught at the instructor's house in a small bedroom which had orange shag carpeting. Each time we arrived for class, I admired the beautiful costumes that were hanging on a rack in the room—most of them richly decorated with beads, sequins, braids, and embroidery. After taking several group lessons with her, I switched to private lessons and became quite good at the dance. To learn more about the dance and its origins, my girlfriends and I attended belly dancing seminars in the Orlando area where we watched professional performers on stage from all over the country.

I was surprised when I learned that belly dancing was created by women for women, to help them during the birthing process.

When my instructor retired, my girlfriends and I joined another class with a teacher named Sophia. During her class, we learned to do a choreographed routine as a troupe. We performed at various local events, and also on stage at the seminars in Orlando. It was exciting being on stage, feeling the heat of the spotlights shining on us, hearing the applause from the crowd as they clapped for every move that we did. Since our instructor worked at the local hospital, she made arrangements for our troupe to perform for some of the patients. I was a little concerned when I discovered that we would be dancing in our costumes in front of the cardiac arrest patients in the recovery room. I was fearful that they may become too excited and have another heart attack. My fears were put to rest when we did our performance and everything went well. After our performance, one of the elderly patients gave me his room number so I could visit him afterwards. Smiling at him, I politely thanked him and told him I was busy.

After learning all we could from that instructor, my friends and I continued our classes from a teacher named Tambil. She taught at the Eau Gallie Civic Center, and had several students in her class. Known as the "Turkish Torch," she was a fascinating woman who originally studied ballet in Instanbul, Turkey, and then decided instead to learn the art of belly dancing. During her career, she danced for famous sultans and also many of the show business greats, including Frank Sinatra, Benny Goodman, and Paul Anka. She even made a number of guest performances on the Merv Griffin Show. A beautiful dancer, with an even more beautiful personality, she was my favorite. My girlfriends and I did a few performances with her at fundraisers for the city of Cocoa Beach.

With belly dancing classes, playing piano, and all my other hobbies, I managed to keep busy while my husband was working with his business up north. Even though we talked on the phone every night, I sensed that being apart was hurting our marriage. Whenever I asked him why he could not move to Florida permanently, he argued with me—giving me the feeling that it was a low priority in his life. Although it was good having his parents around, it wasn't the same as having my husband with me. I was beginning to wonder if he would ever decide to move to Florida to be with me full-time.

─────────{ Chapter 7 }─────────

AFTER EIGHT LONG YEARS OF traveling back and forth, and many months of separation, Donny made the all-important decision to leave the family business—bringing us together again full-time. Having worked with the family business most of his life, it was difficult for him to make this decision. In addition to losing his livelihood, he also had to figure out something new to do with his life. While he was contemplating his new career, he started a lawn care business to keep himself busy. He worked hard at his new business and rewarded himself in the evenings by having a few drinks. Over the next several months, he kept his drinking under control, just like he did when we lived in Massachusetts. When we went on vacations, however, his drinking got out of control and he was not much fun to be with. Every time that we packed for a cruise, he gave me his usual speech about how we could save money during our trip.

"Lisa . . . since alcohol is so expensive on a cruise ship, why don't we take a bottle of rum or vodka with us? That way we can make our own mixed drinks and save tons of money."

Not thrilled with his idea, I told him, "That would save money, but I don't think I'll have a good time if you're going to be drunk during the entire cruise."

"Ah, come on . . . we won't be driving anywhere and we don't have to get up for work the next morning. What's wrong with having some fun on the cruise by having a few drinks?"

The only problem with his plan was that he had all the fun while I had to put up with how silly he acted. Because he drank so much on the ship, we began to argue with each other, which was something we never did before. Not wanting to be alone with a drunk, I made as many friends as I could on the ship and arranged activities to do with them. He became angry when I did this, which usually resulted in an argument.

"What's wrong with you, Lisa? Why do you always include other people when we do things? And why can't you be happy just being alone with me?"

"It's because I don't like being with you when you're drinking. When we were living in Massachusetts, we never argued about anything. And now we argue all the time. And I think it's because you're drinking too much."

"Come on . . . it can't be all that bad. I was just trying to have a good time."

From my point of view, it was bad. And it became so bad that I refused to go on another cruise with him if he was going to drink the entire time. My argument was that he should be able to enjoy being with me without having to drink alcohol. He did keep his promise during our next cruise, but I sensed that he was not having a good time and was bored with everything that we did.

After taking care of lawns for several months, he decided to work with a local family business that manufactured and sold hurricane shutters. He enjoyed being around the owners of the business because they loved alcohol even more than he did. Their names were Bill and Carol. An older couple from Canada, they lived in a cute little townhouse near the beach. They also owned a place in Canada. A three-bedroom lake house, it was situated on a cliff overlooking a crystal clear lake north of Toronto. Whenever they could afford to leave their business for a few weeks, they flew to Canada to stay at their lake house. I was thrilled when they invited us to go with them during the month of August. I loved the huge windows in their house, which provided a panoramic view of the lake. During our visit, Carol cooked some unbelievable meals for breakfast, lunch, and dinner. We ate most of our meals while sitting on the porch at the back of their cabin, looking out at the picturesque lake. The view was magnificent in the evenings, watching the sun as it disappeared behind the trees on the other side of the lake, creating a golden glow in the sky above the trees.

One evening during our visit, we joined them for dinner with friends of theirs who lived on another lake close by. I thought it was pretty cool when they took us there by way of a small boat through the connecting lakes between their houses. The scenery was magnificent as we navigated through narrow passages of water, breathing in the crisp Canadian air, looking up at majestic pine trees towering above us, and spotting an occasional bird flying down from the trees, as if it was going to land right in our boat. We had an amazing time with their friends as we dined with them and then played some interesting card games. Needless to say, my husband and his friends Bill and Carol drank so much alcohol that we could not take the boat ride back home. Instead, their friends had to drive us home in their car.

Once Donny finished working as an apprentice for three years, he stopped working for Bill and Carol. He studied for and obtained a license to start his own hurricane shutter business. During this time, he also gained an interest in local politics and began attending city commission meetings. After attending several public meetings and expressing his opinion on many topics, he took matters into his own hands and ran for office. With a lot of hard work, he was elected as a city commissioner. Not the type of person who enjoyed dressing up for any occasion, he did not own enough suits and had to purchase a few to wear to the commission meetings. Since his father was not used to seeing his son in a suit and tie, he did not recognize him when he saw him on television for the first time, participating in a commission meeting. My husband achieved many goals which helped the city and made his parents and me extremely proud of him. Even though I was proud of him for his many accomplishments, which made the city a better place to live, I was unhappy that he always went to the bar after every meeting to spend time with his new friends. I felt that the only reason he became a politician was to have an excuse to spend more time at the bars. Not seeing him as much, I began to feel lonely.

Donny's father was a great father-in-law. Although he was not overly affectionate, he was a generous man who would give anyone the shirt off his back if they needed it. Many times when we visited his parents, sitting in the front room of their house, watching their tiny television, there were heated discussions between my husband and his father. Regardless of what the subject matter was, they always had an opposite opinion. My husband would say that the sun was yellow, and his father would disagree and say that the sun was orange. As his father became older, he became even more disagreeable and sometimes mean and ornery. Many times he picked on me, sometimes hurting my feelings so much that I cried. It upset me even more when my husband never stood up for me, regardless of how many times his father upset me with the unkind things that he said. He told me just to ignore him and the only reason he said those things was because he was getting old.

When his father was told that he had to have surgery for an aneurysm—a large bubble in his main artery—he became extremely fearful that he was going to die during the operation. On the day before his surgery, Donny's five brothers joined us to visit him at their house. When we were all standing around his father in the tiny room at the front of their house, he became upset with all of us. He yelled at us, telling everyone in the room we were totally worthless, and he had little faith that any of us would take care of his wife Lorraine if he did not survive the operation. Even though we reassured him that we would take care of her, he continued to verbally assault us. He was so mean and spiteful that I had to leave the room because I was crying. On the day of his surgery, I went to the hospital with Donny's mother Lorraine to visit with him before the operation. As soon as we arrived at the hospital, I asked her if I could do something special before we went to see him.

"Before we go upstairs to see Ted, would it be OK if we went into the chapel? I would like to say a special prayer for him."

"Of course it's OK, dear. I was planning on going there myself anyway."

Kneeling in front of the altar, in the tiny chapel at the hospital, I prayed to God: "Please Lord, help this man make it safely through his surgery today without any complications. And by the way, could you also give him a lobotomy during his operation so that he'll develop a better attitude?"

He did survive his surgery and there were no complications. Not being sure if it was either sheer coincidence or my prayer being answered, I was amazed at how much better his attitude was from that point on. He no longer acted like he had a fear of dying and was a lot nicer to everyone. I continued to wonder, for the next several months, what could have caused his miraculous attitude adjustment. Then my sister Gail arrived from Maryland to visit for a few days. During her visit, we decided to spend some time with Ted and Lorraine. After we arrived at their house, my sister began talking about her favorite topic, psychic mediums. I was astonished at what was said by Ted and Lorraine during the discussion.

Gail began the conversation when she said, "I recently attended a John Edward seminar. It's amazing what that man can do. He brought messages through from the other side with so much detail it just boggled my mind."

Lorraine was the first to comment when she surprised me and said, "Oh yes. We have watched his show *Crossing Over* many times. He really is good at what he does."

Completely unaware that either one of my in laws was interested in this topic, my ears tuned in as I continued to listen to what they had to say. Ted spoke up next. For a man who seldom ever spoke about religion, or anything to do with God, I found it hard to believe what he was about to say.

"All that stuff about the afterlife is real. I am certain of it!"

Shocked and amazed by what he just said, I had to ask him, "What makes you so certain that it is real?"

"While I was in the hospital, I had an experience. It happened while I was in the recovery room after my surgery. During that time,

I met the man who opens the gates to Heaven—and trust me—he is for real!"

"Oh my God! How would you describe what you saw?"

"I can't, Lisa. It was too beautiful . . . there are no words that can describe it."

Since we were all intrigued about what he said, we continued to talk about the subject for several more minutes. As my sister and I were preparing to leave the house, Ted added more to what he had already told us.

"Oh. By the way, Lisa . . . I want you to know that the Big Guy asked me to do something. But I can't tell anyone what it is because He made me promise not to."

When he said that, my immediate thoughts were that God must have answered my prayer from the tiny little chapel at the hospital. Several months went by as Ted's health continued to deteriorate. When the time came for him to go, he was not at all afraid. I believe—with all my heart—that he was no longer afraid because he knew where he was going.

With the death of his father, Donny was devastated. Whenever I saw him crying, I tried my best to comfort him with his loss. He ignored me each time that I tried and refused to let me into his heart. Instead of reaching for help from those who loved him, he reached instead for alcohol—just like my father did after my mother died. In addition to drinking in the evenings, he began a new routine of drinking early in the day. Many mornings I watched him as he reached into the kitchen cabinet to grab a bottle of rum or vodka to make his morning drink.

Feeling as if his drinking was pulling him farther away from me, I pleaded with him many times when I said, "Please don't reach for that bottle. Each time that you do, it breaks my heart a little more. I feel like you're choosing that bottle of alcohol over me."

Ignoring my pleas, he continued to do it. When we went to breakfast with his mother on Sundays, there wasn't enough time for him to have a drink before we left the house. Sensing that he was having withdrawal symptoms, I noticed that his hands were shaking when he held up the newspaper to read it. For dinner on Fridays, we stopped going to The Cocoa Beach Pier for our traditional weekly date. I was sad when this happened because I loved going to the pier for dinner, looking out at the ocean from our outside table, listening to music, and discussing all the things that made us happy. Instead of dining there on Friday nights, we went to a restaurant at the bar he frequented after the commission meetings. At this restaurant, he developed a routine where he would sit with me for only a few minutes. He then left me alone at the table while he roamed around the bar area to talk to his friends. Many nights I felt like crying as I felt the pain of being alone, sitting at the table wondering why he did not want to be with me. One night, while I was waiting for him to return to the table, a man from the bar approached me whom I had never seen before. He told me something that I did not understand—at least not at the time when he said it to me.

"Hello, miss. I have something that I need to share with you. I see things sometimes—and I just had a vision that something is going to happen to you. Although it may seem like a bad thing to you when it happens, I want you to know that it'll end up being a good thing for you in the long run." Not saying anything more, he walked away. I never again saw that man come into the restaurant.

The weeks and months went by without any improvement in my husband's behavior. Going to the bars became a nightly event for him. He took me with him whenever he could persuade me to accompany him. On weeknights he sometimes came home late at night. Because I worried about what he was doing at the bar, it was difficult for me to fall asleep. It brought back memories of when my father kept me up late on school nights, telling me his war stories late into the night. I prayed every night for something to happen that would break the terrible pattern that we were in.

In March of 2007, it looked as if my prayers may be answered. When I arrived at work one morning, there was a huge announcement. As part of an Air Force-wide civilian personnel reduction, 15 secretarial positions were being eliminated. Even though my position was not one of them, I was told that I could still be affected. It gave me hope that maybe I could retire early. When Donny and I lived up north, we often talked about the possibility of my job being abolished, which would have given us the freedom that we needed to move to Florida. Just the thought of retirement was enough to excite me—thinking about sleeping in every morning, planning the day however I chose, and never again having to say "Yes, Sir." Since I found a job in Florida, early retirement was no longer something that I thought about—until now. After hearing the announcement, I immediately called the personnel office to find out if I qualified for early retirement. I was given an appointment for the following day to stop by their office to fill out the paperwork.

When I came home from work, I told Donny about my good news. Not completely happy with what I wanted to do, he said, "You do whatever you want, Lisa, but I don't think it's such a good idea. You do know that the longer you stay with your job, the bigger your retirement check will be each month."

"I do realize those things, but this is something I have wanted to do for a long time, and I may never have this opportunity again. And besides, having my life back is more important to me than the few extra dollars I'd be making if I did not retire right now. I really do want to do this!"

He finally told me to do whatever I wanted and he would support me, although I sensed that he was still not happy with the idea. The way that I looked at it, being retired would allow us to do more things together, and it would give us the time that we needed to take the longer vacations we often talked about. Determined to stay the course with what I wanted to do, I kept my appointment with the personnel office the next day, along with several other secretaries. We listened as they explained what to expect with early retirement, and how the process worked for those who qualified and were lucky enough to be selected. They gave everyone an application to fill out. The bottom line was asking for our signature, making a commitment—a commitment that could not be reversed if we were selected. As I looked at that bottom line, it took me exactly two seconds to decide—then I signed it!

Not hearing anything from the personnel office for over a week since I submitted my paperwork, I gave them a call. "Hi. This is Lisa Jones from the 45th Space Wing Safety Office. Over a week ago, I applied for the early retirement program and I have not heard anything since. Can you tell me what the status of my application is?" I was sorely disappointed with what they had to say.

"We're sorry to give you bad news, Mrs. Jones. Since your position includes stenography, there was only one position being abolished that matched yours. We had to offer the early retirement option to another stenographer who had more years of service than you. Unless something unusual happens, I'm afraid your chances now for early retirement are slim to none."

"Please, if anything happens to change that, I would really love to retire."

"We'll keep that in mind. But if I were you, I would not get my hopes up too high."

Although the news was devastating to hear, I did not give up, and prayed intensely when I returned home that night—hoping for a miracle to happen. Two nights later I had an extremely vivid dream that early retirement had been offered to me. The dream was so real that I sat up suddenly in my bed, saying out loud to myself, "Wow! This is wonderful—I'm going to retire!" As I continued to fully wake up, reality set in as I realized it was just a dream. Two days later I received an unexpected phone call from the personnel office.

"Good morning, Mrs. Jones. This is Margaret from the civilian personnel office. We have some exciting news to share with you. Your application for early retirement has just been approved."

Feeling shocked and overjoyed at the same time, I answered her and said, "Oh thank you! That's wonderful news. I'm overjoyed but also a little confused. Just a few days ago, I was told that my chances for early retirement were slim to none. Did something happen to change that?"

"Yes, something did happen that changed it."

I never did find out what had happened, but thanked God that it did. It was like a dream come true for me, and another testament that prayers really do work if you put your heart and soul into them.

When I shared the good news with my husband, he was not as happy as I was, telling me, "That's wonderful news for you, Lisa, but I guess now I have to account for all my time."

"Personally, I think it's a good thing that we're going to have more time together. Maybe we can take some of those longer trips we've been talking about for so long."

"That sounds great, Lisa, but we do have to establish some priorities here. Do you want me to finish fixing the house, or do you want me to leave it the way it is and spend money on vacations? I live in the real world and know that we can't have both."

Even though I chose various priorities and changed them from time to time, the house was never finished, and we never took the longer vacations that we had talked about for many years during our marriage. He continued to pull away from me, finding reasons not to do things together. All he wanted to do was go to the bars, and often dragged me with him even though I protested. During this time period, I asked him repeatedly what his thoughts were about our marriage, and if there was anything that I could do to make things better. Each time that I brought it up, he gave me the same answer.

"No, Sweetie. You're an angel and a wonderful wife. You're not doing anything wrong. It's just me. I don't know what's wrong with me. I just haven't felt like myself lately."

"That's good to know, Honey. I don't want us to become like other couples we know that drifted apart, just because they didn't do enough things together. And then they eventually end up separated or divorced."

"Please don't worry your pretty little head about those things. It will never happen to us."

Being confused with his answers to my questions, I thought perhaps he was still depressed about his father dying the year before— or maybe he was going through some sort of mid-life crisis. I asked him many times to cut back on his drinking. I told him many times that it may be affecting his health and his mood. And I asked him many times to seek help for what I thought was an addiction. I never thought that he would leave me for another woman, but was fearful that alcohol would one day mean more to him than I did. Since he was close to the same age as my father was while I was growing up, he was beginning to remind me of my father. Sometimes when he drank too much, I had flashbacks of my father when he did the same thing, bringing back painful memories of how mean and nasty he used to be. Even though I shared these thoughts with my husband several times, it did not make a difference to him. It was a painful thing to finally realize, but I had grown up with alcohol as a child—and now I was married to it as an adult. It was almost too much to bear.

Since love is blind, I thought he would make it through his drinking phase and go back to being the kind and loving man I once married. Continuing to believe that we would always be together, I did not realize that our marriage was in serious trouble—that is until my eyes were opened as a result of a miraculous event—an event which I believe, with all my heart and soul, was divine intervention.

───────────────(Chapter 8)───────────────

ON NOVEMBER 1ST, 2007, MY sister Gail arrived from Baltimore for our long-awaited cruise. She first mentioned it several months before, but I wasn't sure at the time if it was something that I wanted to do. Sponsored by Hay House, it was titled "The Intuitive Connections Cruise." Since my sister is even more persistent than I am, she eventually persuaded me to join her on the cruise as her cabin mate. With everything that was going on with my marriage, and all the negativity that surrounded me, I was glad that I was going with her. Spending a week with over 300 positive and spiritual people was something that I felt I really needed. The list of speakers for the program that we chose included some of the best in the world on the topic of spiritual growth. In addition to numerous inspirational talks, my sister told me we would have the opportunity to hear messages from the "spirit world." Even though I had my doubts about where those messages really came from, I decided to go with an open mind, and looked forward to whatever experiences would unfold for me during the next seven days. I also saw this cruise as an opportunity to spend time with my big sister whom I dearly loved.

My sister Gail is the oldest of the six children in our family. An attractive brunette with hazel eyes, she is a wonderful, loving person who I cannot say enough good things about. She was like a second mother to my younger sister and me while we were growing up, teaching us how to do everyday things like brushing our teeth properly and showing us how to take a shower instead of a bath. When my parents were drinking, she was always there to pick up the slack for things that they failed to do. Most holidays were happy occasions only because of her love and generosity. When she received her paycheck from her government job every two weeks, she always spent at least half of it on buying household items for the family or purchasing toys for the children. My favorite childhood memory—which happened one Christmas morning—is a prime example of the thoughtful things that she did for us. Two days before Christmas, I was devastated when I lost my Thumbelina doll. I searched everywhere in the house that I could think of but I could not find it. Feeling sad, I was hoping that Christmas morning would bring me something special to cheer me up.

When Christmas morning arrived, I was eager to open all my presents. Waking up before any of my brothers and sisters, I hurried down the stairs to the living room where the Christmas tree was. As I sat under the tree to search for my presents, I had to brush away the silver tinsel that became tangled in my hair. Excitement filled me as I began to pick through the many presents, searching for the ones that had my name on them. Some were marked from Mom and Dad, and others were marked from Santa Claus. After I opened a few of my presents, I picked up a package the size of a shoebox. As I tore off the wrapping paper and opened the box, tears of happiness filled my eyes when I saw what was inside it—my old beaten up Thumbelina doll, cleaned up and wearing a gorgeous new dress. What I saw on that day, when I looked at the beautifully transformed doll in the box, has always served as a symbol to me that anyone can be transformed with enough love, prayer, determination, and courage.

After Gail and I arrived at the cruise terminal in Ft Lauderdale, something unusual happened while we were waiting in line to check in. When several Hay House authors arrived at the same time—and rode up the escalator together—it suddenly stopped working. The check-in process was delayed for several minutes while we waited for the elevator to be repaired for an electrical problem. As I stood there and looked at the elevator, I remembered something interesting about energy and electricity. It was something my sister told me about after she attended a John Edward seminar. She said he thought it was funny that he had to replace numerous microphones that shorted out, most likely due to the psychic energy that surrounded him when he was doing readings. An interesting thought to ponder is that several spirits may have been around the mediums on the escalator, and it is possible that their energy could have caused the escalator to stop. I am not sure if it's true or not, but it is a strange coincidence that makes you think.

Our cruise was scheduled to take us to the Eastern Caribbean with stops in the British and US Virgin Islands. The speakers for the cruise were all Hay House authors—Gordon Smith, John Holland, Sonia Choquette, and Colette Baron-Reid. I was not familiar with the speakers before going on the cruise, but after hearing them speak, I was extremely impressed with what they had to say. Besides seeing them in the seminars, we were able to speak to them socially whenever we ran into them during the course of the cruise. We had an opportunity to speak with all the speakers except for one: Gordon Smith. Known as the "Psychic Barber," he is hailed as Britain's most accurate medium. My sister told me we were extremely fortunate to have him as part of our program. Whenever we did see him, he was usually hanging out at the bar and had fans swarming around him, making it difficult for my sister and me to approach him for questions.

In addition to the seminars with the Hay House authors, we were entertained by the excellent shows after dinner each night—choreographed with beautiful singing and dancing, and complete with music emanating from a full orchestra. As an added surprise for us, one of the dancers in the show happened to be the daughter of one of Gail's friends. Her name was Monica and she was absolutely beautiful. You could tell that her parents were proud of her just by the way they looked at her during her performance. They had no idea that she was going to be performing on the ship until just a few weeks before the cruise. I was very much impressed with the charisma she displayed on stage. Considering how much movement there was from the seas rocking the ship, it was amazing that she didn't fall or trip while she performed some of her moves.

Every night in the dining room, we sat at a different table and met all kinds of wonderful people who shared the same interests. With Holland America being known as the Culinary Cruise Line, the food that they served was beyond delicious. One of the best meals that we had—and definitely the most interesting—was when my sister and I went to a special lunch one day, and it was purely by accident that it happened. For the first two days of the cruise, we dined at the buffet for our lunch. As we were heading to the buffet on the third day, an idea popped into my mind that we should try the dining room instead.

Thinking that my sister may also like the idea, I looked at her and said, "Why don't we do something special today and eat lunch in the dining room? I think it'll be a nice change if we eat there instead of at the buffet."

After she agreed with my idea, we proceeded to the main dining room. When we arrived at the entrance, standing before us were all the ship's senior officers, including the captain of the ship. As we walked by them, each one of them greeted us, shook our hands, and then told us who they were. Since it was my first time on a Holland America cruise, and I thought that meeting the ship's officers at lunch was their normal routine, I said to Gail, "Wow! They really go all out for their lunches on this ship."

We entered the dining room and were seated at a long table with several other people. Shortly after being seated, the wine steward came by and began pouring wine into our wine glasses. Since wine is typically an extra charge on most cruises, I asked, "Did someone order this wine for us?"

He politely responded and said, "No one did; the wine is complimentary."

"Thank you sir, that's very nice. This is the first cruise I've ever been on where the wine is complimentary at lunch."

Then they served our lunch, which was prime rib with all the trimmings. By this time we were wondering if perhaps we had wandered into a special event, uninvited. It finally dawned on us that we did when we noticed a special gift of a fancy wine stopper placed at each table setting. When we confessed that we were there by mistake, the waiter told us not to worry about it and to enjoy our lunch. We eventually learned that the event we attended was Holland America's welcome back luncheon for guests who had cruised with them before.

In between meals and going to shows, we attended the speaker presentations. During one of the sessions with John Holland, he asked for a volunteer to do an experiment with him up on stage. Along with several other people in the audience, I put my hand up. Excited when he chose me, I proudly walked up to the stage. As a safety precaution, I was asked to remove my high-heel shoes so that I would not trip or fall off the stage due to the movement of the ship. The experiment began when I was instructed to hold my arms straight out to the side so that he could test my strength by pushing down on them.

When he was not able to move my arms, using all the strength that he had, I proudly said, "I'm probably pretty strong because I've been working out with a personal trainer for several months."

"I can see that. You do have some muscles in your arms. We're going to try this exercise again but I'll be placing a blindfold on you first."

He placed the blindfold over my eyes and walked around me, explaining to the audience that he was breaking up my aura. My sister told me later on that he was making an up and down chopping motion with his hands. He then asked me to hold my arms out again. This time my arms had no strength and he was able to easily push them down. After that, he walked around me again and did something to put my aura back together. Once that was completed, we did the experiment again and my strength had come back to me. It was amazing!

While he was removing my blindfold, I was hoping that I would receive a message—just like the last two people who went up on stage with him. When he did not say anything, I asked, "Is anyone trying to send me a message?"

I was disappointed when he looked at me and said, "No, they are not."

After spending six wonderful days in the Caribbean, our cruise was soon coming to an end. My sister was correct and the Hay House speakers were nothing short of phenomenal. They increased our awareness of the spirit world and put us in touch with our own higher self. Although I did not receive any messages of my own, it was amazing to hear some of the messages given to other people in the audience. The accuracy of the details, which the mediums provided to members of the audience, was enough to convert just about anyone into a believer who did not believe before. All my doubts had been removed; leaving me thoroughly convinced that our loved ones who have left this world can communicate with us. My only disappointment was not hearing anything yet from my mother, and it was the last night of the cruise. Since Gail wanted us to have good seats for the last session of our program, she went to the auditorium early while I returned to our cabin to freshen up a little.

As I sat alone in our cabin, thinking about all the great speakers we had already heard, my thoughts turned to our final speaker— Gordon Smith. He was doing the last seminar of the cruise and I knew it would be my final chance at hearing from my mother. For over 24 years I had wondered who she was speaking to when I last saw her, who she was with in Heaven, and how she was doing. Every time I shared the story of that last meeting with her, it brought tears to my eyes. According to readings my sister Gail and other family members had received from other mediums, we never heard from my mother because she was always in the background, never strong enough to come through on her own.

Before leaving the cabin to meet up with my sister in the auditorium, I sat on my bed and spoke out loud to my mother.

"Mommy, I would love to hear from you. If you could just say something, anything, get over to the edge, or whatever you need to do, I know he'll hear you because he's really good. I would like to know who you were talking to when I sat by your bedside the last time that I saw you. I also want to know who you're with in Heaven, and most importantly, how you're doing and if you're OK."

I sat on my bed a few minutes longer, praying and thinking about my mother. Then I left the cabin and headed down to the auditorium. When I arrived, there were over 300 people from the Hay House group sitting in the audience, eagerly waiting for Gordon to take the stage. After spotting Gail with an empty seat next to her, I walked over and sat down beside her, wishing—with all my heart—that I would be one of the lucky few in the audience to receive a message from Heaven.

When the session began, Gordon explained how the readings worked and what to expect. Within minutes there were spirits coming through with messages for several people in the audience. I was astonished at the details that he shared with each person who received a reading. Referring to relatives they had lost, he gave their full names with middle initials, names of streets they had lived on, and several other details which were amazingly accurate. He then asked for a volunteer to go up on stage to assist him with a reading. Excitedly, I put my hand up. To my disappointment, he picked someone else. Her name was Bea and she was extremely excited to go up on stage with Gordon. When she arrived on stage and stood beside him, he laid his hand on her shoulder. He explained that he did this so she could see what he was seeing and assist him with the reading.

He began his exercise by asking the woman next to him what she saw. She told him that she saw a hospital and an image of an arm. I listened closely as he began to describe the exact scenario of what happened just before my mother's death. He spoke of a woman in a hospital who had suffered a stroke on her left side. He said she did not die suddenly, but had been taken to the hospital, and he felt as if she didn't live very long after she got there. This was the moment when I realized it had to be my mother he was talking about. Not saying a word to anyone, I thought to myself: It's Mommy! She did have a stroke on her left side, she was taken to the hospital by my father, and she lived only a few days after she got there.

Then, Gordon pointed at me and said, "I'm drawn to you, the lady in the black sweater who wanted to come up here on the platform."

And then someone handed me a microphone.

Tears filled my eyes as I quietly said in shock, "That's my mother."

After I confirmed that it was my mother he was speaking about, he asked her to give her daughter a memory. Between him and his assistant, they said that she was showing them blue shoes, and I was asked, "Do blue shoes mean anything to you?"

When I told him I could not figure it out, he asked, "Can you understand where there was something awkward going on with your mother's feet near the end of her life?"

"Yes, there was. She complained a lot about her feet being swollen because her circulation was bad. She could not get enough blood into her feet which caused them to turn blue."

Gordon then went on to say that it was her mother, who was my grandmother, who was waiting for her before she passed. I was completely amazed since this was one of the questions I had asked her just minutes before, while I was alone in my cabin. Instead of an angel floating above her in the hospital, it was her mother who must have asked her if she was ready to go to Heaven.

I replied by saying: "When I last saw her in the hospital, she was speaking to someone, but no one else was in the room with us. I assumed that it was an angel, and then I told her to go to Heaven."

He told me that she was thanking me for telling her that. He also said that he felt as if she would have never had any great mobility or use if she had lived.

Amazingly, the next thing that he said answered my second question: "Who is with her?"

"There is a photograph of a man, who as a child had blonde hair, which I am seeing. This is a man in the spirit world with her. I am seeing somebody who was young and fair-haired as a young man or a young boy, but that's just how your mother remembered him. She remembers him as being fair-haired as a young man, but he died as an old man, not as a young boy."

Quickly responding, I said, "But my father had black hair!"

After a few chuckles from the audience, he said he did not mean to start a family argument and quickly changed the subject.

As I thought about the photograph that he spoke about, I wondered if it had anything to do with the man my mother dated before she met my father. Based on what I had heard before, I was aware that spirits often provide evidence through readings that can be verified at a later time. They do this to provide reassurance to whoever is receiving their message that it is real.

The next part of the reading was something that completely took me by surprise. I did not figure it out until after I went home and shared it with my husband.

Gordon asked the woman who was assisting him with the reading: "Ask her mother if there was just one word her mother could say to her, just one word. Ask her for something. Give me a word, anything you would like to give to your daughter, right now from Heaven."

After thinking about it for a few seconds, she said, "ring."

Gordon looked at me and went on to say: "Can I ask you to thank her for that, because I feel that the ring is important to you. That symbol is very important to you. It's almost like this unity, something that is continuous that will sustain you in your life that will be continuous and lasting. There have been too many things in your life that have gone out of your life too soon. I feel as though that symbol, that ring, is actually more to do with something that is lasting and eternal."

Since I had been married for over 22 years to someone whom I thought was a good husband, I responded to his comment and said, "My marriage to my husband is very good."

Gordon surprised and confused me again with his answer.

"But there is something your mother is bringing in that is saying she wants to see you get into something that is continuous in your life—something that goes on and on and on. She is giving it as a positive symbol."

He ended the reading by saying that she was not suffering any more, and when you are in a coma like she was, it is much easier to pass to the other side. This was the answer to my third and final question: "How is she doing?"

When the seminar was over, I was still curious about the photograph of the man who was in the spirit world with my mother. Thinking that the woman on stage with him may have also seen it, I asked her: "I am very curious about something that was said during the reading. Did you happen to see the photograph that Gordon spoke about?"

"Yes, I did."

"Wow! Can you tell me more about it and what it looked like?"

"Yes, I can. It was a black-and-white photograph of a little blonde boy. And he was wearing a white shirt with long puffy sleeves."

"Thank you so much for sharing that with me. That photo may have something to do with the man my mother dated before she met my father. A few years ago I bought his autobiography, and I can't wait to check out all the photos in it when I get home."

When my sister and I returned to Cocoa Beach, I immediately searched the house for Daniel's autobiography. After I found the book, I took it into the living room to look through while my sister rearranged her suitcase. Hoping to find a photograph similar to the one that Bea described to me, I opened the book. As I slowly turned the pages, I came to the part of the book where Daniel was a young boy. Suddenly, I had goose bumps! On the page I was looking at, there was a black-and-white photograph of a young boy. His hair was blonde and he was wearing a white shirt with long puffy sleeves. At that moment, I recalled something interesting that occurred after I had purchased the book. Because the book was not available at the local bookstore, I had to order it. The day it arrived for me was the same day that a friend called to tell me he had passed away—as a very old man.

Eager to share the photograph with my sister, I took the book into the bedroom to show it to her. "Gail! You have got to see this photograph that I found in Daniel's autobiography."

"Let me see. Oh my God! That is exactly the way Bea described it to you. Mom knew that you would find that photo. That's her way of letting you know that she's still with you."

My sister finished packing and then I drove her to the Orlando airport to catch her flight back to Baltimore. After I dropped her off, I had some time to think things through during my drive back to Cocoa Beach. I thought about everything I had heard during the session with Gordon, and how most of it made sense to me—my mother's feet turning blue, her mother waiting for her in Heaven, and the man in the spirit world with her. I was a little confused, however, about what my mother wanted me to get into that would be eternal. My first thought was that maybe she wanted me to get another job since I was retired. That would make sense, except for the part about it being something continuous that goes on and on. And then I thought about how he brought it up again after I told him my marriage to my husband was very good:

"But there is something your mother is bringing in that is saying she wants to see you get into something that is continuous in your life—something that goes on and on and on. She is giving it as a positive symbol."

The one person I knew who could give me some insight into the meaning of the message was my husband. Although I was eager to share it with him, I sensed that his response may not be something I wanted to hear. I decided to wait until the right moment to share it with him.

──────(Chapter 9)──────

WHEN I RETURNED TO THE house, Donny was home and greeted me when I walked through the front door. Although he looked happy to see me, I sensed that something major had changed with him while I was away. With each day that went by, he appeared more and more distant to me, and he was reaching for the alcohol in the kitchen cabinet more often. My gut feelings were telling me that our marriage was not on solid ground, as if it was sand sifting through my fingers. On the weekends, the only time we spent together was when we went to his favorite cigar bar. While he sat at one end of the bar drinking whiskey with his drinking buddies, I sat at the other end playing the video machine. The virtual poker players on that machine were the only friends I had at the bar. By focusing on playing the game, it enabled me to block out everything that was going on around me.

On Saturdays and Sundays, I saw very little of him because he was never home. I could understand him not being home on Saturdays, but not having him home on Sundays puzzled me. Since the beginning of our marriage, Sunday was always our special day to do things together. Because he always had a business to run, he worked on Saturdays—with his power equipment business in Massachusetts, with his hurricane shutter business in Florida. I was used to being alone on Saturdays and spent that time catching up on my chores and housework. What I was not used to—and I was not happy about—was not having him home on Sundays.

After not seeing him for several Sundays, I finally decided to ask him about it and said, "Sweetie, I haven't seen you much since I've been home from the cruise. Can we do something fun together on your day off next Sunday?"

"I'm sorry. I'm going to be busy on Sunday. I already made plans to go golfing with my friends."

"What about next Sunday?"

"I can't go then either. I'm going to be golfing on Sundays for the next several weeks."

Totally confused and hurt, I looked at him and said, "You cannot be serious. Sunday has always been our special day together for as long as I can remember. Are you telling me that you're taking our Sundays away from me? I cannot believe you're doing this to me."

Without even hesitating, he answered me and said, "Yes, I am. It's something I want to do."

Very hurt, and not knowing what to say back to him, I just walked away. I thought that maybe he was still depressed about losing his father and needed some time to be alone.

As Thanksgiving Day came closer, we discussed plans for our holiday dinner. I was not thrilled with the plan that he came up with.

"Lisa, for Thanksgiving this year, what do you think about having dinner at the bar with all our friends? You won't have to cook anything because the owners of the bar are willing to prepare all the food."

"Well, that may be a good idea for you and your friends, but we usually have dinner that day with your mother. Personally, I don't think it's the right place to share a holiday meal with your mother. Have you discussed this idea with her?"

"No, but I will. I don't think it'll be a problem."

"There's no way it will not be a problem! I absolutely disagree with this idea and plan on cooking dinner myself at home."

"Okay. I can go along with that . . . whatever makes you happy. We'll have two dinners. Early in the afternoon, you can cook dinner at home. After that dinner, we'll eat again at the bar."

It was no surprise to me at all when his mother fully agreed with my opinion. When Thanksgiving Day arrived, I prepared a delicious turkey dinner with all the trimmings, similar to the dinners my mother used to cook while I was growing up. Knowing how much Donny always enjoyed my turkey dinners, I spent hours in the kitchen preparing the meal for him and our guests. His mother Lorraine, as well as a few of our friends, joined us for dinner. Since some of our friends did not have family in the local area, I thought it was a nice gesture to share the holiday with them. While everyone was seated at the table and putting food on their plates, I noticed that Donny was fidgety. It was obvious that he absolutely did not want to be there. After he piled a huge mound of mashed potatoes on his plate, my friend Kim passed the plate of turkey to him. I could not believe it when he said, "No, thanks. I don't want any of that." Before we even said Grace, he began eating his potatoes while he kept looking at his watch. Just minutes after finishing his meal, eating only the potatoes, he stood up from the table and headed toward the front door.

"Listen . . . when you're finished here . . . give me a call and we'll meet up at the bar."

In a hurry to leave the house, he bolted out the door, almost slamming it behind him. After cleaning the dishes, I visited with my friends and then played a few card games with his mother, Lorraine. Once everyone left the house, I gave him a call. When he answered the phone, I could tell by the sound of his voice that he already had several drinks. Dreading the thought of spending the rest of the evening with him at the bar, I reluctantly put on my happy face and spoke to him.

"Hi, Sweetie. Your mother just left the house and everyone else has gone home. I should be at the bar to meet you in just a few minutes."

His response to me was shocking—not at all what I expected to hear. "Don't even bother! I've already eaten and now I'm at the strip club. And I know you don't like it here. What took you so long to call me anyway?"

"What are you talking about? I was playing cards with your mother."

I could not believe the way that he spoke to me and the things that he said—especially since I had been entertaining his mother. After arguing with him for a few minutes, I became angry and upset and told him, "You are not being fair to me! Please come home."

"No. I'm staying here."

"Do you mean to tell me that you'd rather stay at the bar than be home with me on Thanksgiving?"

"Yes, I am. I would rather stay here."

Shocked and upset, I suddenly realized that he had just turned his back on me and our marriage. With tears coming out of my eyes, I felt the sadness even more as I thought about my mother who had her first heart attack on Thanksgiving Day. I absolutely did not want to be alone and pleaded with him one more time.

"Please come home. This is the saddest day of the year for me and I don't want to be left alone."

Sounding like he could care less how I felt, he said, "Stop your crying and don't be getting so upset. I promise I'll come home after I have a few more drinks." And then he slammed the phone down.

As I sat on the edge of the bed crying, memories of my father came into my mind: In a dingy bar with my brothers and sisters, patiently waiting to go home, our father would tell us, "One more drink and I promise we'll go home." After thinking these thoughts, I cried even more as I asked myself: What is happening to my husband? He has never spoken to me like this before.

After I cried myself to sleep, I was awakened a few hours later by the creaking sound of the front door when he opened it. As I listened to the sound of his footsteps coming down the hallway, I shuddered as he approached the bedroom door. I pretended to be asleep—shielding my heart from hearing anything more that was mean. As he crawled into the bed with me, I wondered to myself, with a feeling of deep sorrow: What happened to the sweet, kind man that I married?

The next morning he apologized for his behavior from the night before. He explained that he did not know what was happening to him, and promised that it would never happen again. He was very sweet to me the entire day, telling me how much he loved me and how special I would always be to him. During the day, he was completely different than he was at night when he drank—which was exactly how my father used to be.

The following night was probably the worst night of my entire life. When he left the house in the late afternoon to do volunteer work at the Cocoa Beach Art Show, he promised to call me when he was finished. Knowing that his volunteer assignment was to work at the beer booth, I did not put much faith into hearing from him anytime soon. As he walked toward the front door to leave the house, he looked at me and said, "After I finish working, I'll give you a call. We'll get together and listen to whatever band is playing tonight."

A few hours later, my girlfriend Jamie stopped by the house to visit me. Someone I had known for many years, she was the craziest friend that I had. She was petite with blonde hair and had a great love for music. When she played her guitar and sang for the residents at the local nursing homes, she said it brought her joy when she saw the smiles on their faces. In between working and playing her music, she had three teenage sons who kept her busy. When Donny was working up north, she and I did a lot of fun things together.

When I told her I was waiting for Donny to call me so that I could meet him at the art show, she made a suggestion and said, "Why don't I go with you? We can leave early and surprise him."

"That's a great idea, Jamie. We'll leave right now."

When we arrived at the downtown area where the booths were, we were the ones who were surprised. We walked over to the beer booth, where he was supposed to be working, and discovered that it was empty. After we asked a few of the other workers what had happened, we were told that they shut it down early because there wasn't enough business to keep it open. A little confused, I could not understand why he did not call me earlier to let me know. We searched through the crowd for my husband and then looked in the bar where he usually hung out. When we entered the bar, it was dark and dreary with a dense cloud of smoke in the air. This was the place where my husband spent most of his time, hanging out with his drinking buddies. After we were there a few minutes, my friend

Jamie described the bar as "The Den of Iniquity." Not seeing him there, I continued to search for him outside while my friend Jamie visited some of her friends that she saw earlier.

Eventually, I returned to the bar, thinking that he would be there. As I searched through the crowd in the bar, I did not see my husband anywhere. I did find his best friend, who was married, kissing some woman who was obviously not his wife. Not wanting to be involved with the situation, I left the bar and continued my search outside. After several minutes with no sight of him anywhere, I reluctantly returned to the bar to see if his friend was available to answer any questions. Since his lady friend had left, I asked him if he knew where my husband was.

"He's outside. I'll go get him for you."

Before I could tell him, "I will get my husband myself," he quickly ran out the back door. When he returned a few minutes later, my husband was right behind him. From the way that he looked, it was obvious he had been drinking for hours and was thoroughly consumed by alcohol. As I looked at him closer, his eyes were bloodshot and empty-looking, as if he wasn't even there. After looking at me for only a few seconds, he staggered past me to a chair, sat down, and began sobbing like a baby. I tried desperately to talk to him.

"Are you OK? Why don't we go outside and listen to the band? I think the music might help." After arguing with him for several minutes to persuade him to go outside, he reluctantly stood up and walked with me.

We were outside for only a couple of minutes when he panicked.

"Oh no! I left my cell phone in the bar. I need to go find it."

"That's OK. I'll go help you."

Stopping me dead in my tracks as I tried to follow him, he abruptly turned around and said, "No, Lisa. You stay right here and wait for me. I'll be right back!"

He walked away and left me standing all alone in the middle of the street. When he did not return after several minutes, a sick feeling came over me. I could sense that something evil was happening. Luckily, my friend Jamie returned to help me out. I asked her to find out what happened to him—too afraid to find out for myself. As I waited anxiously, she went into the bar to search for him. Five minutes later I saw her returning with my husband. They were walking so fast that they were almost running, as if each of them were trying to reach me first. Looking totally disgusted with whatever he had been doing when she found him, she walked some distance away, yet kept an eye on me as I dealt with my drunken husband.

When I tried to talk to him to find out what was going on, he began screaming at me, causing a scene, telling me over and over again: "Please go find Jamie, Please! You have to find her and ask her to go home with you!"

"No! You are the one who needs to go home with me. You have had way too much to drink tonight and you're not acting like yourself. What is wrong with you?"

"I don't know what's wrong with me! All I know is that I want to be alone tonight. Just go home and let me be alone! I'll spend the night in my van and I'll see you in the morning."

He wasn't making any sense to me at all. Before I could say anything back to him, he ran away from me, disappearing into the crowd, leaving me alone again in the street—extremely angry and confused.

After he left, my friend Jamie returned to talk to me. Still fuming about what she discovered, she said, "I caught him red-handed! He was behind the bar, and he was standing in front of a woman. It looked like he was kissing her!"

"Are you sure about that? What did she look like?"

"I'm not too sure. She was much shorter than him, kind of petite with brown hair. He had her pinned up against the side of the building. I couldn't see her face."

"It sounds like she may be the same woman that I saw in the bar earlier. She was in the bar kissing his best friend. I wouldn't worry about it too much."

In an attempt to block out the emotional pain that I was feeling, I tried to convince myself that nothing serious was going on. Thinking that she was just a part of the bar scene that he was involved with, I tried desperately to forget about it. The longer I tried to close my eyes to it, the more painful it became for me. As an attempt to try and pull myself together, I changed my thoughts to something more positive. I focused on the message from my mother that I received on the cruise. The part of the message that was unclear to me before was beginning to come into focus. It was the response Gordon gave me after I told him that I had a happy marriage to my husband.

"But there is something your mother is bringing in that is saying she wants to see you get into something that is continuous in your life—something that goes on and on and on."

Standing there in the middle of the street, feeling as if I was all alone in the world, it was obvious to me that my marriage would not continue much longer. Reluctantly, I went home to an empty house and tried to go to sleep. Not being able to fall asleep, I tried calling him several times on his cell phone. He would not answer his phone. Even though it was after midnight, I decided to drive back to the downtown area and search for him. I was hoping that I would be able to find him sleeping in his van and talk some sense into him. After I parked my Toyota 4-Runner, I started walking through the streets of downtown Cocoa Beach. The recent red tide outbreak was dreadful that night, with thousands of dead fish washed up on the beach. Because of the onshore wind that picked up the microscopic algae from the fish, the toxins in the air caused my eyes to sting as tears streamed down my face—the pain of the sting adding to the emotional pain that I was already feeling. Walking through the streets after midnight gave me an eerie feeling. There wasn't a person in sight anywhere, except for one lonely security guard. He was watching over the closed-up vendor tents from the art show. Continuing to search for my husband, I could not believe what was happening to me. I grew up with alcoholic parents, and now realized that the man I married had turned into an alcoholic. Living with alcohol had become a terrible pattern in my life—repeating itself again—this time taking away the man whom I thought would love me and be with me forever.

The next morning he came home just after sunrise. For the second day in a row, he apologized by saying that he did not know what was wrong with him, and promised he would never do it again. I asked him about the woman in the bar, and he reassured me that he did not remember kissing anyone that night. Because I still loved him, I believed him.

The following night he decided to stay home with me, but still drank a lot of alcohol. Thinking it was time, I decided to share the message with him that I received during the cruise. I persuaded him to spend some time with me in our hot tub so that we could talk. After waiting several minutes for him to join me in the hot tub, I banged on the window to the room he was sitting in, thinking he may have forgotten that I was waiting for him outside. A few minutes later he staggered out of the house, carefully holding a drink in his hand, and climbed into the tub with me. Once he sat down in the warm water, I attempted to start a conversation with him. I became angry with him because he was focusing only on his drink, ignoring everything that I was saying to him. Trying to catch his attention, I grabbed the drink out of his hand, threw it on the ground, and shouted at him, "Listen to me!"

As I started to gain the strength to tell him my story, I looked into his eyes. They were dark and empty looking, as if his soul had left his body. The soul temporarily leaving the body was a topic of discussion from one of our seminars on the Hay House cruise. If you abuse your body through drugs or alcohol, the soul does not like that type of environment and may leave your body temporarily, connected by an invisible thread, until your body returns to normal. It was a mind-chilling experience to see it first-hand.

Gathering my strength, I began to speak. "I'm not really sure how to tell you this, but while I was on the cruise with my sister, I received a message from my mother. Ever since I came home from the cruise, I've been trying to figure out the meaning of her message. I'd like to share it with you and hear what your thoughts are."

He did not say a word but was still listening to me. I continued with what I had to tell him. "She told me that she wanted me to be happy and to get into something more continuous. She is sending me a gift, straight from Heaven, which is supposed to be something eternal that goes on and on. My thoughts on this message are that maybe you'll get better and will continue to love me forever, or maybe someone else will be coming into my life. Can you tell me what you think?"

My heart was pounding as I looked into his dark empty eyes, anxiously waiting for his response.

"I'm sorry you had to hear that from a dead person . . . but I'm not happy being at home and would rather be at the bar with my drinking buddies."

His response literally broke my heart and shattered it into a million pieces. Feeling an unbelievable pain come over me, it was as if my heart was being ripped apart, piece by piece, and my entire world was crumbling around me. Fighting back the tears, I looked deep into his eyes and said, "You cannot mean that! How can you say such a thing to me after all these years of being together? Do you realize that you just broke my heart?"

Looking at me as if I meant nothing to him, and showing no remorse at all, he said, "It seems like we aren't even married any more. You never want to go anywhere with me, and when we do go to dinner, we don't talk anymore."

"That's because you're drinking most of the time, and the only places we ever go to lately are the bars and the strip clubs. I don't go with you because I despise those places!"

All he had to say to me was that he was sorry and then he went into the house for another drink. I went to bed, and again cried myself to sleep. The one thing that helped me to make it through that night was the hope that my mother had given me through her message—and the thought that somehow she was going to take care of me with her special gift from Heaven.

Morning arrived, and he asked me, "Why are your eyes so red? It looks like you've been crying all night long."

"Don't you remember what happened last night? You broke my heart with all the mean things that you said to me."

After reminding him of everything that he had said to me, he apologized again. This time he sounded as if he really meant it.

"Oh, Honey. I'm so sorry I said those things to you. Please don't cry. I did not mean any of it. I promise you, this will never happen again."

As much as I wanted to believe him, I found it difficult considering what he had said to me the night before. The emotional damage had already been done. Thinking back to the mean things that my father used to say when he was drinking—and the fact that he never remembered the next day that he ever said them—I came to the realization that my husband had become exactly like him.

During the next few weeks, he was on much better behavior, perhaps finally realizing how much he had hurt me. We talked a few times and came to an agreement to work on our marriage together. Even though he agreed to what we discussed, I still had the feeling that we were drifting farther and farther apart. For the third week of December, we had plans to fly to Baltimore to visit my family. It was something that we did every year, except for the times when we could not make it due to bad weather. A few days before our trip, he decided not to go with me and cancelled his plane reservation. He never explained why. After asking him several times why he changed his mind, he went into a temper tantrum—and with a frown on his face, he looked at me and said, "I really don't want to go!"

We made it through the next several days without much turmoil— at least until Christmas Eve. A few days before Christmas, he told me that we were going to the strip club for their holiday celebration on Christmas Eve, instead of going to midnight Mass with his mother. Just like the year before, I tried to change his mind about going, but with no success.

"I really don't want to go this year. May we please stay home and go to Mass with your mother like we used to do?"

"We have to go! All my friends will be there. And besides, they're giving away some really cool prizes. The owner of the bar told me today that I'll probably win a large screen television. I just know we'll win something really big."

"What about the smoke? You know that it hurts my eyes and they sting like crazy in that place."

"Don't worry about that. They'll have smoke eaters and we'll be in an area just for VIPS which will be roped off."

"Your mother is expecting us to go to midnight mass with her. Are you going to disappoint her?"

"Of course not. We'll leave the bar around 11:30, take her to mass, and then take her back home and go back to the club. You see, everything is all worked out."

The longer that I argued with him, the more upset he became, eventually crying like a baby until I agreed to go with him. When we arrived at the strip club, he brought me over to the VIP area that was roped off and showed me where I could sit down. Then he left me there, telling me he had to talk business with some of his friends and he would be right back. As the night went on, he did visit with me a few times, but he spent most of his time talking to his friends. I was not at all surprised when they had the big drawings and he did not win a single prize. When it was time to pick his mother up for midnight mass, we left the bar and went home to clean up a little.

As we sat in the church with his mother—on the holiest night of the year—I tried to ignore the stale smell of smoke from the bar that was still on our clothing. Listening to the choir sing beautiful songs with angelic voices, it was such a strong contrast to the place we had just left minutes before. His mother knew where we were before we picked her up for mass, but she was such a saint that she said nothing about it. As a saving grace, he did find it in his heart to drop me off at the house and returned to the bar by himself.

When he was not drinking during the day, he was nice to me and pleasant to be around. He continued to tell me that he did not know what was happening to him, and that we would work on doing more things together. A few weeks later, we went on a cruise with another couple from Massachusetts. Something magical happened on that cruise—something that gave me the hope that everything was going to be OK.

(Chapter 10)

ON FEBRUARY 8, 2008, OUR friends Joe and Jean arrived from Sudbury, Massachusetts. The purpose of their trip was to visit Donny's parents, Ted and Lorraine. When they planned it several months before, they extended it by a few days so that they could go on a cruise with us. This was going to be our second cruise with them. The first cruise that we took together was early on in our marriage. It was a special trip, sponsored by the Toro Company, for their best power equipment dealers in the New England area. When we made plans to cruise with them again, everything seemed OK with our marriage at the time. We had no idea that it would take a turn for the worse in the months leading up to the cruise. Even though I sensed that Donny did not want to go on this trip, he had no choice. Since he did not want our friends, or his mother, to know that our marriage was in trouble, he had to make an attempt to act like everything was normal. Always trying to look at the good side of things, I thought the cruise may help our situation since he would be away from his friends for a few days—friends that had a terrible influence on him. And if things did not go well on the cruise, I felt good knowing that Joe and Jean would be there if I needed emotional support or someone to hang out with.

Joe and Jean were an interesting couple and a lot of fun to be around. Jean was a patient, easy-going French woman. She had a heart of gold and always saw the good in everyone. Her husband Joe, on the other hand, was a crazy Sicilian. Although he was a generous man who would help anyone who needed it, he sometimes became overly excited during conversations with his wife. Watching them interact with each other was always entertaining. They could be yelling at each other one moment—looking as if they were in a knockdown, drag-out fight—and a few moments later everything would be back to normal, most likely because Jean was forgiving and had the patience of a saint. In addition to thinking about spending the next few days with them, I thought about the last time that we cruised together. The four of us had never cruised before, and were extremely impressed with our experience. My husband and I were so spoiled by the time that the cruise was over that we ended up booking several more throughout our marriage. We had a great time on every cruise that we took after that one, except of course for the few occasions during cruises when he drank too much alcohol.

After Lorraine drove us to the port, we checked in and proceeded to board the ship. As we stepped onto the ship and walked through the atrium, my thoughts turned to memories of the good times that Donny and I shared during all our previous cruises. I was hoping to recreate some of those memories, giving us what we needed to possibly start putting our marriage back together. After giving our friends a quick tour of the ship, we all headed to our cabins to unpack our suitcases. We then met up with Joe and Jean and headed to the buffet for lunch on the lido deck. Somehow on the way to the buffet, my husband disappeared. I ended up having lunch with our friends, wondering to myself: What the heck happened to him? Focusing my attention instead on having something good to eat, I joined the line at the buffet to pick out my food. There were many entrees to choose from, as well as a scrumptious salad bar, several vegetables, freshly baked breads, and a variety of desserts. The food looked absolutely delicious and lifted my spirits, even though my husband was not there to share it with me.

Shortly after getting in line, I noticed a tall gentleman standing behind me. It completely took me by surprise when he said, "Hi. How are you?"

Being the outgoing person that I am, seldom does anyone ever say hello before I do. As I turned to look at him, I was quite surprised at how I felt when I gazed into his eyes. Looking very familiar to me, I had the strange feeling that I had met him a long time ago, but could not figure out where or when. He was tall and handsome with dark hair, and had a smile that touched my heart the moment that I looked at him.

In response to his question, I politely answered him and said, "I'm fine. Thank you."

With nothing else being said between us, I walked over to my table and sat down to eat my meal with Joe and Jean. After I sat down and put my tray on the table, I told them, "Wow! The cutest guy just came up to me and said hello. And it made me feel really good." I looked over to where he was sitting and noticed that he had a woman with him. She did not look too happy, but it was apparent that they were traveling together.

The next morning, the four of us arranged to meet for breakfast at the buffet where we had lunch the day before. We weren't even halfway there when Donny had to run back to the cabin for something he had forgotten to bring with him. He told me to go ahead and he would catch up to me in a few minutes. Since I was starving, I joined the line at the omelet station as soon as I found the table where Joe and Jean were sitting. While standing in line, I asked several people where they were from. It was my way of starting conversations with new people that I met on the ship. Whenever I talk about cruising to my friends, I always tell them: "It's not necessarily the ship you are on that makes it a great cruise. It's the people that you meet and the interesting conversations that you have with them." As I waited for my omelet, I looked up. Standing in front of me was the man I had met the day before. Trying to start a conversation with him, I said, "Hi. Where are you from?"

With his beautiful eyes, he looked at me and said, "Tampa."

Curious about the woman that he was having lunch with the day before, I had to ask, "Are you traveling with family?"

I thought his response to me was interesting when he said, "Just friends."

Again, nothing more was said between us. Since my husband still had not returned from the cabin, I joined my friends to eat breakfast with them. Sitting at the table, I was wondering to myself: What could he forget in the cabin that is so important it couldn't wait until after he had breakfast with me?

The cruise went on for a few more days as I continued to find myself either alone or with Joe and Jean most of the time. Each day Donny kept finding excuses to be away from me, and I had no idea where he went or what he was doing. He even walked out of the after-dinner shows a few times, telling me how bored he was. He had an unhappy look on his face most of the time, and was definitely not the joyful person I remembered from all our previous cruises together. His strange behavior was giving me an uneasy feeling. To help fill the void that I was experiencing, I found myself continually looking for the man I had met at the buffet—my spirits being lifted each time I saw him. One of those times was during the welcome back celebration for guests who had cruised more than five times with Royal Caribbean. The room had an elegant setting with beautifully sculpted ice carvings, sparkling on a buffet table covered with small bites of food—as if we hadn't eaten enough food already that day. A small band was playing beautiful music, creating a romantic atmosphere that inspired me to want to dance. The bad thing for me was that free alcoholic beverages were available to everyone present—which my husband was taking advantage of in a big way.

After we had been sitting at the table for a while, I looked at Donny and said, "The music is putting me in a dancing mood. Would you like to dance with me?"

Holding a drink in his hand, nervously swirling it around, he looked at me as if he was irritated that I had even asked him such a thing. "Maybe we can, but it'll have to be after I have a few more drinks, which might just put me in the mood. But to be honest with you, right now I don't feel much like dancing."

Since I really wanted to dance, so that I could be held by him, I asked him several more times. After he had a few more drinks, he reluctantly agreed and we made our way onto the dance floor. As he held me during the dance, almost stepping on my feet because he was drunk, I glanced over his shoulder to the other side of the room. The man I met at the buffet was sitting with his girlfriend on the far side of the room, looking right at me. It was the only moment that I enjoyed during the entire dance.

On the last night of the cruise, while we were enjoying a delicious dinner in the dining room, thoughts of the man I met came into my mind. Wishing that I would have just one more opportunity to see him, I thought to myself: If it is meant to be, it will happen. After we finished eating dinner, my husband and I left the dining room and began walking toward the theater for the after-dinner show.

We were just outside the dining room when Donny suddenly stopped and said, "Listen. I have a bad headache, so I'm going back to the cabin. Why don't you go find Joe and Jean and see if they'll go to the show with you?"

Reluctantly, I said, "OK. I'll go look for them and will see you later tonight in the cabin." After searching for a while, I finally found them, only to be disappointed when they told me they were going to the casino instead. Not wanting to go to the show alone, I decided to take a stroll around the ship. And then I headed toward the casino. Just like my mother, Amelia, I loved to play the slot machines.

As I strolled toward the stairs in the center of the ship, my heart skipped a beat as I saw him again. There he was—the man I had met at the buffet who had been on my mind throughout the entire cruise. He was standing in front of the stairs—looking straight at me. An unforgettable moment, I felt as if I were in a scene from the movie *Titanic* as I slowly walked over to introduce myself. As I stood before him, I felt a strange sensation, and my body began to tremble as I spoke to him. "Hi. It's nice seeing you again. It's so interesting that we keep running into each other like this. My name is Lisa. What is your name?"

With a beautiful smile on his face, he shook my hand and said, "It's nice to keep running into you too, Lisa. My name is Steve."

Still feeling the trembling sensation, I continued to talk with him for a few minutes. I told him a little bit about my husband, and then talked about my job with the Air Force. He talked about his girlfriend and told me about his job at the police academy. When he mentioned the military base where he worked when he was in the Air Force, I said, "Wow! I used to work with a General Lilley in Maryland who transferred to that base in the 1980s. He almost hired me to work for him as a secretary. I even visited his office to do a job interview."

I was shocked and amazed with his response when he said, "I remember him—I worked in his office for a very long time."

A strange feeling suddenly came over me as I thought to myself: Oh my God! I may have actually met this man when I went for that interview. It could be the reason why he looks so familiar to me. I wonder how different my life would be today if I had been given that job working for the general. It was such a crazy thought that I did not mention it to him. I pondered how amazing it was, and how one small event in your life can change things dramatically. I wanted to keep in touch with him, but did not know how to tell him.

Since I was good at sales, I quickly came up with something to say. I asked him, "Does your girlfriend use Mary Kay products?" When he said he did not know, I reached into my pocketbook to give him my business card. "If she does, I just happen to be a Mary Kay consultant and would really appreciate the business. My phone number and e-mail address are on this card."

As he walked away, it took all the strength that I had not to run after him, asking him to e-mail me anyway. As I stood near the stairs for a few moments, thinking about our conversation, I could hear piano music playing somewhere in the background, possibly from the deck below. I strolled over to the stairs and leaned over the railing where I could see the piano player. As I stood there listening to the music he was playing, I felt a profound beautiful feeling come over me. Unlike anything I had ever experienced before in my life, it felt as though a white light were shining down on me—directly from Heaven—giving me an unbelievable feeling of peace and tranquility. The feeling was right around my belly button, also known as the solar plexus. I stood there for several minutes listening to the music from the piano player, enjoying the moment, not wanting the feeling ever to stop.

When the piano music did stop, I walked around the ship for a few minutes longer and then headed back to our cabin. When I opened the door to the cabin, my husband was already asleep in the bed, most likely passed out because he had too much to drink. Reluctantly, I crawled into the bed with him. As I closed my eyes and thought about my beautiful experience, I had a smile on my face, and a feeling of peace, that I had not felt for a long time. I knew with profound certainty that somehow everything was going to be OK—and I would one day be loved again.

When the ship returned to Port Canaveral, Lorraine picked us up and drove us home. When we arrived at our house, a strange feeling came over me when I opened the front door and looked into the living room. It felt as if I was literally being attacked by the clutter that was in the house. Even though the same clutter had been in our house for many years, it was the first time that it ever bothered me. The feeling was overwhelming; as if something was telling me that it had to be removed. Thinking about how I was going to remove all the clutter from my house, and not knowing how or where to begin, I turned it over to God and asked him for help.

Two days later, I went to visit my friend Bonnie who lived in a beautiful beachfront villa in south Cocoa Beach. Her home was magnificent, designed by her husband Patrick who was an architect. Whenever I paid her a visit, I always admired the Italian marble flooring throughout their house. She is who I would refer to as the "Voice of Reason." A tall woman, with flaming red hair and a perfect body, she was a realist who always saw things for what they were. Her responses to some of my questions were usually blunt, but almost always the truth that I needed to hear. During our visit, I told her about the clutter situation at my house and asked her if she had any ideas on how I could take care of it.

"Of course I do. I never told you this before, but I love organizing other people's homes, and quite frankly, I'm pretty good at it. As a friend, I would love to help you out."

"Wow! That is such a nice thing for you to do. What I am about to tell you may sound a little strange, but just two days ago I prayed for some help with my clutter situation."

"Good deal. We'll start tomorrow if you have time."

For the next several days, she spent hours with me. We went through every room in the house, every closet, every cabinet, and every drawer.

Each time that we went through a pile of stuff, she asked me: "Do you really need this stuff, or do you think someone else can enjoy it?"

Except for a few items which I refused to give up, everything that we went through was either put into large garbage bags for the trash, or loaded into my car to be donated to a local charity. By the time we were finished, I felt energized—as if I had just received a cleansing. Another benefit was the new energy that I felt each time that I walked through my front door. Thinking about the huge difference that it made, I thought to myself: If I could do the same thing to my personal life, perhaps it would allow more positive energies to flow into it.

My husband was pleased with how the house looked, and gave a lot of thanks and credit to my friend Bonnie for helping me. Being on a little better behavior, he made an effort to make things better for our marriage by cutting back on his drinking. When I finally came up with the courage, I asked him about the woman he was seen kissing at the bar.

"I've been wondering about that night when my friend Jamie said she saw you kissing someone at the bar. Was it just a drunken mistake, or is there something else going on between you and her?"

"No . . . nothing is going on between us that you need to worry about."

In response, I told him that I believed and trusted him and wanted to do more things together. Thinking about the 24 years that we had been together, I did not want to throw it all away without trying. Even with that being said, I still had an uneasy feeling that our marriage was becoming worse instead of better.

Another reason I did not want our marriage to fail was because of the friendship that I had with his mother, Lorraine. She was an incredible woman, and much more to me than just a mother-in-law. I had known her almost as many years as I did my own mother before she died. If things did not work out between her son and me, I was fearful that I would lose her friendship. She lived only a few blocks from our house, which made it convenient to visit her. When Donny and I went to see her, he always sat in the front room and watched television while she and I played cards at the kitchen table. Almost every time that we played cards, we asked him if he wanted to join us. He always gave the same response: "Next game, I'll play." Even if his brother Bobby and his wife Donna stopped by the house to play cards with us, Donny still refused to play. Many times he fell asleep while he was watching television. We could always tell when he was asleep because we heard the commercials playing—knowing that he was not awake to change the channels like he normally did.

Even though she was in her 80s, his mother beat me at cards nearly all the time. Her mind was extremely sharp and her eyesight was perfect. She did not need to wear glasses for anything. She loved playing cards, and just like me, she loved playing bingo and the slot machines. When her husband Ted was alive, they took many trips to the casinos in Biloxi, Mississippi, during the time that they lived in Florida. A few weeks after the cruise, I invited her to join me at one of the many video arcades in the area, Ocean O'Aces. When we arrived at the arcade, my friend Davin was serving Chinese food for lunch. As part of our lunch, we were each given a fortune cookie for our dessert. Lorraine ate her cookie first, after she read her fortune.

When I pulled the little piece of paper out of the cookie that I was given, I was puzzled when I looked at the words that were written on it. Thinking it was unusual, and that I should share it with Lorraine, I read it to her out loud: "*Be prepared for a sudden, much needed, happy change of plans.*" I was completely oblivious to the fact that the following day that fortune would come true in a big way.

(Chapter 11)

THE NEXT DAY MY FRIEND Bonnie called and invited me to play a game of *Scrabble* with her. After a short drive to her beachfront home, I walked up to her front door and rang the doorbell. As I waited for her to answer the door, I thought about how strange it was that she invited me over with such short notice. It was out of character for her. She normally planned everything that she did well in advance. When she opened the door, I could tell by the look on her face that something more was going on than just a visit to play *Scrabble*.

"Hi, Lisa. Thanks for stopping by today, even though I didn't give you much of a heads-up. Why don't you come into the living room with me and sit down? There's something I need to tell you. And I think it'll be better if you're sitting down when you hear what I have to say."

After entering her huge foyer, we walked through her kitchen, and then entered the huge living room where we sat on her European-designed white cotton sofa. As I listened to the sound of the ocean waves coming through the sliding glass doors to her back porch, I could also hear the sound of my heart as it was beating. I sensed that what she was about to tell me would not be good news.

It's difficult for me to tell you what I need to say, Lisa . . . but I have good evidence that your husband has been seeing another woman."

"Are you sure about this? Even though he's been acting strange lately, I did not pick up on any clues that he was seeing anyone else. How do you know this is true?"

She went into great detail about how blatant he was about the whole thing, not caring if anyone knew or not, and informed me about how long it had been going on. It came as no surprise to me when everything that she described took place while he was either drinking at the bar, or late at night after he left the bar. When she finished with everything that she had to say, I looked at her and said, "Thank you. You just set me free."

I had wondered at the time why I said those words, but realized why down the line. It was what I needed to hear to be able to finally open my eyes, and to set myself free from a man who loved alcohol more than he loved me. We talked for a while and played a game of *Scrabble*. It was not easy for me to focus on the game with the many thoughts that were racing through my mind. I thought about what I was going to do when I got home, and if I should mention it to him right away. I also wondered if the person who told her all these horrible things was telling the truth. As we played our *Scrabble* game, I felt a terrible pain growing in the pit of my stomach. After we finished playing the game, we talked a little more.

Before I left to go home, she told me, "Maybe it's best that you don't say anything to him about this right away."

As I drove my Toyota 4-Runner back to the house, I managed to keep my emotions under control. I was doing OK until I walked through the front door and entered my kitchen. At that moment, I lost all control of my emotions and began crying. For the past 24 years of my life, he was always the first person I talked to when I had a problem, or if I was upset about anything. Feeling like I had to talk to him right away, I picked up the phone and dialed his number. When he answered, and I heard his voice on the other end, my voice shook as I spoke to him:

"Hi. It's me. I just heard some disturbing news and I'm not feeling too good at the moment. I really need to see you so we can talk."

"I'll come home right away. I'll be there in just a few minutes."

It seemed like forever as I stood in my kitchen and waited for him. When he arrived at the front door, he was sober and had a serious look on his face. Before he could say anything, I asked him, "Can we please go into the living room and sit on the sofa before we talk?" He grabbed my hand as we walked into the living room. After we both sat down, I told him what I had heard and asked him if it was true. With a heartbreaking look on his face, he began to speak.

"I'm so sorry about all of this. I want you to know that everything that's happened is entirely my fault, and you have done nothing wrong. I don't know what's happening to me, Lisa, and I have no excuse for my behavior or how I've been treating you lately. You deserve so much better than this."

There was a terrible pain in my stomach as I tried to talk some sense into him. "But we had so many happy years together. Why can't we go to counseling? If we do, maybe we can find out what's wrong with you, and then we can fix our marriage. I know we can make everything work out if we try." My heart ached even more when I heard his response to what I said.

"No! We cannot go to counseling. The first thing they'll ask me to do is to give up drinking. And I cannot do that."

It was totally heartbreaking and gut-wrenching, realizing at that moment that my prior prediction from years ago had come true. Alcohol had become more important to him than our marriage. It made me think about the time when I asked my father to stop spending money on alcohol and cigarettes. Even though I asked him so he would have more money to spend on school supplies, he yelled at me. He told me it was something he enjoyed and those were things that he would never give up. Then my thoughts turned to Donny's mother, and the possibility that she may never want to see me again if I divorced her son.

"What about your mother? Once she finds out what's happening to us, I'm afraid that I may lose my friendship with her. I love her so much and I don't want to lose her."

As he broke down in tears and put his hands over his eyes, he said, "Oh God! I don't want that to happen. I'll make sure she knows this is all my fault and you are not to be blamed for anything."

Trying desperately to think of something to keep him from leaving, I brought up the issue of health insurance. "If we end up being divorced, you'll lose your health insurance. What will you do then?"

I was quite surprised at his answer when he said, "It would be very selfish of me to stay with you, making you even more miserable than you already are, just so I can have health insurance."

"I don't understand why you have to move out of the house. Why can't you stay here and maybe things will work out after a while?"

"If I stay in this house with you, I'll just continue to come home drunk every night. And I know that doesn't make you happy. Leaving you is the best possible thing that I can do for you right now. You're a beautiful woman, and you have a wonderful, loving personality. I cannot think of a reason why any man would not fall madly in love with you. I really hope that you can find someone nicer than me, Lisa—someone that you can be happy with."

After our conversation, he got up from the living room sofa and walked out the front door—never again to spend another night in our home. After he was gone, I sat there and stared at the door in total disbelief, trying to ignore the aching pain that was growing in my stomach. I thought again about the hope my mother had given me through her message. I used that hope to gather the strength that I needed to start putting my life back together.

In retrospect, looking back on this moment—for a man who I often thought was selfish because he never wanted children—giving me my freedom that day was probably the most unselfish thing he had ever done for me.

(Chapter 12)

THE NEXT SEVERAL DAYS WERE long and painful as I tried to sort through my thoughts. Feeling like I was all alone in the world, not knowing which way to turn, I decided it would be good to leave town for a few days so I could think things through clearly. I made arrangements to visit my friend Jamie on the west coast of Florida. She had recently moved to St. Petersburg, which was close to one of my favorite spots—Venice, Florida. Having been to Venice many times, I knew it would be the perfect place to put my thoughts together for starting a new life. Nestled between Sarasota and Fort Myers, Venice is a relaxing beachside paradise located directly on the Gulf of Mexico. Just the thought of going there made me feel better, thinking about swimming in the warm waters of the gulf, strolling down tree-lined Venice Avenue, and walking past the quaint, colorful shops in the historic downtown area.

During the three-hour drive across the state, I listened to music to soothe my mind, playing songs like Frank Sinatra's *Come Fly With Me* and *I Did it My Way*. As I approached the neighborhood where Jamie lived, I admired the stately buildings with Spanish architecture surrounded by clusters of tall palm trees and large Norfolk Island Pines. The house that she lived in was a small two-bedroom that she shared with her teenage son, David, and her beautiful black cat whose name was Mr. Bud. During my visit, we did lots of fun things together in the evenings, but during the day I ventured out on my

131

own while she went to work and her son went to school. I began each day by eating breakfast at the Cracker Barrel. Since the morning temperatures were a little chilly in the month of February, I always chose a table near the fireplace. While eating my breakfast, I felt the warmth of the fire as I gazed into the mesmerizing fireplace. With each flicker of the flames, I could feel the pain of my broken heart slowly melting away, giving me the peace that I needed to sort through my thoughts. It was a new start for me; the healing process of mind, body, and spirit had begun.

The second day after I arrived, I visited Venice Municipal Beach. I felt like a child again, swimming in the warm water, jumping up and down with the waves, and then floating on my back as I gazed up at the cloud formations in the sky. Unlike most beaches on the west coast of Florida, it was one of the few that had wave action. When I finished swimming, I spent the rest of the day doing something that intrigued me most about the beaches in the Venice area—searching for the prehistoric, fossilized shark's teeth that wash up on shore. Looking for the fossils has always been my favorite hobby, and it served me well that day. Although I enjoyed finding them while walking on the beach, it was more adventurous searching for them in the water. Using a wire basket attached to a wooden stick, I first had to go into the water and scoop out the sand with the black rocks. Then I shook my wire basket vigorously in the water to remove the sand—leaving only rocks, shells, and fossils in my basket. After dumping my catch onto my beach towel, I sat down to search through the pile. Using my fingers to sift through the rocks and shells, I looked for the shiny black teeth, as if I were searching for gold. It was so relaxing that I could do it for hours at a time.

During this visit, I thought long and hard about moving across the state to live in Venice, leaving my old life behind me in Cocoa Beach. The dream house that Donny and I had built was now a constant reminder of the alcohol and sadness that destroyed our marriage. All I wanted to do was sell my house, move away, and begin a new life with new surroundings. On the third day of my visit, I met with a realtor in Venice to discuss the possibility of buying a home there. I looked at a few places and fell in love with a cozy little condo. Located within walking distance to the beach, it was a ground-floor unit located right next to a lovely marina. It looked like a peaceful place to live.

Before leaving to come home, I thought about Steve, the man I met on the cruise ship. Still fascinated with the idea that I may have met him many years ago, I wanted to talk to him about it. Because I knew he worked at the police academy in Tampa, I gave them a call. After calling a few departments in the academy, I finally reached him and was able to speak to him.

"Hi, Steve. You may not remember me, but my name is Lisa. I met you about a month ago on the Soverign of the Seas."

"Of course I remember you, Lisa. It's good to hear from you. How are you doing?"

Not wanting him to know my current situation, I did not mention what was going on in my personal life. "Everything's good with me. The reason I called is to ask you about doing a tour of the academy. I'm visiting a good friend of mine in St. Petersburg this week and have some extra time."

"I would love to give you a tour, but I'm extremely busy right now with my work. How about keeping in touch with me through e-mail and we'll arrange it at another time when you visit your friend again."

"That'll work. I'll keep in touch with you, Steve"

I continued to keep in touch with him over the next few weeks, hoping that he would have time for the tour. After a few weeks of e-mailing, I eventually told him that I was separated from my husband, explained what I was going through, and shared the beautiful feeling that I experienced when I last saw him on the ship. His response to me was kind and helpful, providing me words of encouragement and advice. I will always treasure his thoughtful words. They helped me immensely and were the spark that I needed to speed up the healing process. This is the e-mail that he sent me:

Hi Lisa,

Thanks for sharing your thoughts and the kind words; it is evident you possess courage and determination, and these attributes are essential for success. I have no doubt you will find what you are looking for.

As much as I appreciate your apology, there are no apologies necessary. It seems as though I was there for you at a time when God was trying to tell you something, and I was merely the messenger. Many of us have found ourselves in similar circumstances, and the strong have managed to break away from the destructiveness and overcome the hurt to pursue a relationship that has meaning and worth. I am glad I could be that band-aid for you, as you are in the process of re-discovering yourself and determining (what and whom) makes you happy and successful. Since we are in two different places in life (as I have already walked a mile in your shoes), you need this time to figure out what direction is best and go there, as life is not a dress rehearsal.

I do wish you the best, and remember it is a slow process that requires a lot of patience. Good things come to those who wait, and your best days are still ahead of you. Take care and have a great day!

Steve

From that point on, I referred to him in my mind as the "Messenger" and still wondered who or what would be the "Gift" that my mother was giving me from Heaven. Over the next several weeks, we continued to keep in touch and he sent me additional beautifully written e-mails with more words of inspiration and encouragement. A few times he suggested that I read books written by Joel Osteen. The first book that he suggested was *Become a Better You*. It was amazing and even talked about divorce, saying how sometimes it is unavoidable; but when one door closes, God will open another if you keep the right attitude. My belief in God and the spirit world helped me more than anything else to make it through this painful period of my life.

In the month of March, my friend Jamie and her son David came to visit me for a few days. During their visit, Jamie and I made arrangements for her friend Della Danley to visit my home and apply her magic through the art of massage. A phenomenal massage therapist as well as intuitive counselor, she was extremely helpful with my healing process. During my massage session with her, she counseled me intermittently with her soft-spoken voice. When I told her I was not certain which direction in life I was headed, she guided me through my emotions and gave me phenomenal insight as to where I should concentrate my focus. When we discussed the separation from my husband and pondered how devastating it was, she presented me with a beautiful analogy:

"Your life is like a piece of pottery. It starts out as a fragile piece of clay, and then it becomes stronger when you put it through the fire. Just like the piece of clay, Lisa, you have been put through the fire, and it will also make you stronger."

"That is beautiful, Della. Thank you so much for sharing that with me."

"You are most welcome, Lisa."

When we talked about self esteem and the feeling of self love, she said, "You will know that you have reached the point of self love when you can sit in a quiet room all alone, and say to yourself, *I love you.*"

During the next two months, Donny and I talked about whether or not we should file for divorce, but neither one of us hired an attorney nor took any action. He did apologize many times for how he hurt me. However, I had to remind him that there were two other parts to an apology that he neglected to include—the first being "I am sorry," the second, "Can you forgive me?" and the third, "How can I make it better?" With that being said, I knew there wasn't much hope in putting our marriage back together. It hurt me even more that our marriage of over 22 years was not important enough for him to go to counseling.

Many of my friends encouraged me to hire an attorney. Because Donny was so agreeable to anything that I wanted to do, I felt like I did not need an attorney. When I became tired of listening to my friends constantly bugging me about the subject, I finally consulted with an attorney for legal advice and did research on the internet about the divorce process. I began concentrating on the required paperwork, but took my time in finishing it. Even with all that had happened to me, a part of me still believed that a miracle would come into my life, and everything would go back to the way that it was. Having this mindset made it difficult for me to let go, which was something I really needed to do to move forward.

In early May, I went to see a psychic medium and counselor in the local area named John Rogers. After listening to many of his lectures at the Cocoa Beach library, I decided to book a personal session with him at his home in Melbourne, Florida. I liked his candid, straight-forward attitude. He began my session with a puzzled look on his face when he said, "Are you married? The reason I ask is that I sense this up and down thing going on with you."

I responded and said, "Yes, I'm married. But, I'm currently in the process of filing for divorce."

He went on to say that my husband turned his back on my marriage and it was not my fault—exactly what Donny told me the day that he moved out of the house. He talked about my father and said that he wanted to make a small apology for how he treated me when I was growing up, and that he would make a bigger apology later on. Then he talked about my mother and said that she would stay with me the entire time until I was feeling better.

With another puzzled look on his face, John asked me, "Did your mother have a second husband or a boyfriend? I ask because I don't see her hanging out with your father. She's hanging out with some other guy. Your father is actually hanging out with the guys, and sometimes his own father, which is your grandfather."

"That's interesting that you should say that. My mother did have a boyfriend before she met my father whom she loved very much." Then I added, "And when my father was alive, he always did like hanging out with the guys and drinking with them."

John came to the obvious conclusion that since my father was an alcoholic and my husband had a drinking problem, I had married my father. I thought it was humorous when he added that I was a drunken Roman soldier in one of my former lives. I was thrilled when he told me that I was finished with alcohol in my life and would be moving forward.

When I told him my plans to move to Venice Beach, Florida, his response was not something that I wanted to hear. "I don't see you living there. You'll most likely settle somewhere out west near the state of Arizona."

"I don't understand. I don't even know anyone west of the Mississippi. Even if I did know someone in that part of the country, why would I want to live near Arizona? My plan is to move to Venice, Florida as soon as I can."

"I'm sorry, Lisa. I just don't see that happening."

When I asked him if I would be working again, he told me that he did not see it and instead saw me in a classroom setting learning something fun. He advised me to file my divorce paperwork as soon as possible and told me that I should be feeling much better around August.

Then he said, "Your husband will try to win you back. I see him giving you red roses. Although I normally encourage reconciliation when someone is thinking about divorce, your situation is different. I advise you not to take him back because he will never change."

At the end of our session, he asked me if I had any questions for him. Then I told him that I met a man on a recent cruise and was wondering if I would ever see him again. Not giving him any more details, I was surprised at how he described him when he asked, "Was he tall with black hair? And was there something special about his eyes?"

"Yes. He was very tall with black hair. And when I looked into his eyes, I felt as if I had known him from somewhere else. Do you think I will ever see him again?"

"He is helping you right now. You may have a romance with him, but not until later on. I also feel as if you and this man were together in a prior life."

As I was leaving his house, I had to ask him, "I am curious about one thing. What would Don's father Ted say about this situation if he were alive today?"

After thinking about it for only a few seconds, he responded with, "He's a nice guy, Ted. He's the sort of guy who would give you the shirt off his back if you needed it." Looking at me again—as if he were baffled—he asked me, "Is this his son we're talking about?"

"Yes. It is."

"He is saying to walk away."

I recalled the warning Donny's father gave me the day before I left Florida, telling me that his son was a blooming drunken idiot. It suddenly made complete sense to me. I was thinking at the time that his father was just a funny guy, but I realized now that he was trying to warn me about his son's drinking problem. Close friends of the family told me that Donny's father threatened his son when he discovered that I was leaving Florida to be with him.

They said that he told him, "This girl is leaving Florida to be with you. If you do not make sure that she's happy, I'll take the family business away from you and give it to her."

With that being said, I often thought that once his father was gone, the marriage might fall apart. There would no longer be any accountability to his father, and he would stop trying. Sadly enough, I believe that is exactly what happened. My husband strongly disagreed with me when I shared these thoughts with him after he moved out of the house.

When I returned home after the reading, I called my best friend Tracy to tell her all about it. After telling me she had always wanted to have a reading with a medium, she suggested we take a trip to the Cassadaga Spiritualist Camp, just north of Deltona, Florida.

Established as a spiritualist community in 1894, it is the oldest active religious community in the southeastern United States. One of her friends highly recommended we visit a woman who lived there by the name of Hazel West Burley—a spiritualist medium as well as a counselor. Agreeing that it would be an adventurous and fun thing to do, we made plans to take a day trip. After driving an hour-and-a-half through the Florida countryside—to a town so tiny that you would miss it if you blinked your eyes—we finally arrived. The moment we turned off the main street, our anticipations piqued. As we drove down tree-lined streets, we passed several quaint Victorian cottages, and noticed some of the local residents walking their dogs.

After we drove around the town for a few minutes, we visited the only hotel in Cassadaga. Walking into the hotel was like stepping back in time as we looked at our surroundings. We were told that the hotel had been renovated to preserve the quiet elegance of traditional sophistication which was common for hotels during the 1920s. After touring the hotel, we had lunch at the Lost in Time Café, and then walked across the street to the bookstore and information center where we met some of the local residents of the Camp. Everyone that we met said they enjoyed living there and that it was peaceful. They told us that although the residents owned the homes that they lived in, the church owned the property. And even though the word "Camp" appears in the name of their community, there are no camping facilities available.

We then drove to Hazel's home, which was where she did her readings. After driving through a wooded area in search of her house, we found it and parked in a grassy area which we thought might be her front yard. She lived in a pink wooden cottage with white trim and a white picket fence. When we walked toward her front porch, we noticed the beautiful flowers that were everywhere around her house. As we stood on her front porch and rang the doorbell, I thought about the many things we may hear from her. In addition to being a medium, she had a background in psychology, and specialized in helping others with their emotional and relationship difficulties. What she had to offer was something I felt I really needed. When she opened her front door, we saw a kind-looking woman with dark hair and a tiny brown and white shih tzu at her feet. While trying to stop her dog from barking, she greeted us with a soft-spoken voice.

"Please come in, Tracy and Lisa. It's such a pleasure to meet the two of you. Don't mind Bilbo Baggins. He'll calm down in a few minutes."

We walked into her living room and sat on her sofa while she talked about her background and described what to expect during our sessions with her. We were asked to write a few sentences on a piece of paper because she used our handwriting to understand our spiritual identity and qualities. Before our readings began, she explained that they may take a little longer than planned because she does not like to rush her readings. She told us that time stands still when she is with her clients.

Before we began our sessions, Hazel asked us, "Which one of you would like to go first?" Since Tracy never had a reading before, I told her, "I think Tracy should go first since this is her first time."

I thought it was cute when the little dog followed them into the room. Hazel told us that the dog thinks he is the medium but he usually goes to sleep during the readings.

When Tracy came out of the room over an hour later, I could tell by the look on her face that she was happy about her session. I was excited for her when she said, "Hazel suggested that I take up ballroom dance classes. She said if I did, I would meet a man on the dance floor who would sweep me off my feet."

"That's a great idea Tracy! I would love to take dance classes with you. As soon as we get home, let's look into scheduling some. It would be a good thing for me because I would have the romance of dancing with men without having to deal with the dating thing right away."

As I was walking into the reading room, I overheard Hazel asking Tracy if she would like to take Bilbo Baggins for a walk through the neighborhood. When I entered the room, I immediately sensed the peaceful feeling created by the lavender walls and drapes, and the beautiful purple rug on the floor. My reading began when my father came through to give me a huge apology for how he treated me while

I was growing up. I thought it interesting that during my reading with John Rogers, a few weeks before, he mentioned that my father would give me a bigger apology at a later time.

Then Hazel told me something about my father that really hit home with me. It helped me to understand why he was never close to me or any of my brothers and sisters. "He is telling me that back then the mother was the one who stayed home with the children and was close to them, and the father hung out with the guys—and that's just the way it was."

My mother came through next. Hazel asked me if my mother died from a heart condition. When I asked her how she knew, she said that she can feel how people die when their spirits are around her. She said her heart began fibrillating when she felt my mother's spirit.

"Your mother wants you to know that she and your father are proud of the way you are handling things in your life right now. Also, she's telling me that having her last two children took a toll on her, but she did love all of you very much."

"Thank you for sharing that with me Hazel. I do remember my mother at times telling me how having children can have an effect on your health. She also told us that she loved us and never regretted having any of us."

Then Hazel spoke about something that was dear and close to my mother's heart.

"Your mother is sharing something with me that she hopes you can remember. It has to do with a time during her life which she says was the happiest she ever was. Does the letter 'H' mean anything to you as it relates to your mother?"

"Yes, it does. She must be referring to the man that she dated before she met my father. He was an intelligent man who created a successful business, and the name of his company began with the letter H. She talked about him all the time, telling me how much she loved him. Does this mean that my mother and father are not together? Even though they had some alcohol issues, I do know that my parents loved each other."

Speaking with a kind voice which was also comforting, Hazel said, "Of course your mother and father are together. When you are in the spiritual dimension, love is not the same as it is here on earth. You can share your love with many people. There are no feelings of jealousy."

Then Don's father, Ted, came through, having a lot to say. He spoke for himself, as well as his wife Lorraine, who was still living.

"Ted is telling me to let you know . . . although they welcomed you into the family when you married their son, they always felt that you deserved better. He wants you to know that they have something special for you. It is something that they feel will be better off in your hands than their son's."

Then her facial expression changed and she had a serious look on her face.

"I don't mean to scare you or anything, but they are telling me that you need to take everything that is yours and put it in your name only. They fear that their son is going to be involved with some bad financial situations that could affect your assets. They do not want you to lose anything because of what he does."

I thought what she said was interesting. Just before Donny and I separated, we mortgaged one of our rental houses so that he could open a bar with his best friend—who was also his drinking buddy. Thinking the obvious—that two drunks opening a bar was not a bright idea—I was very much against it. He disagreed with me and screamed and cried until I agreed to sign the papers. I took Hazel's advice after I returned to my home and changed everything that I owned to my name only. I was glad that I did because his business venture ended up as a total failure, which caused him to lose everything that he invested. If I had not taken her advice and removed his name from my assets, I could have lost everything that I owned.

She continued on with the reading, reassuring me that if my husband were well again I would be the one he would love. She also said that when I see him in the next dimension of life, I will feel the love that we used to share but it will be in its true form.

"That's wonderful to hear, Hazel. Speaking of love," I asked haltingly, "do you think I'll be meeting anyone else in the near future?"

"Yes. You will definitely have a new man in your life . . . and he will be very, very nice. You will be unbelievably happy!"

"Wow! Are you sure about this?"

She looked me straight in the eyes and said with great certainty, "I can guarantee it!"

"When will this happen? Is there anything that I need to do?"

"No. You do not need to do anything. It will evolve on its own."

We left her house feeling really good about the session we each had with her. The ride home was fascinating as we discussed everything we were told and what some of our relatives had to say. In particular, we were thrilled about scheduling our dance classes—Tracy being more excited than I was, thinking about the possibility of being swept off her feet on the dance floor. Even though we were eager to schedule our dance classes and begin taking them, we had to wait a few weeks. My sister Gail was arriving in a few days from Maryland. She was scheduled to take a cruise on the Disney Wonder with her daughter Valerie and grandson Joey.

It was wonderful having my sister and her family visit with me for a few days before their cruise. When Donny stopped by the house on one of those days to pick up some personal belongings, it created an awkward situation with my sister and her family in the house. After he left the house, my sister and her daughter Valerie told me, "This is so sad. And he doesn't even look like the Donny that we used to know." Having my big sister to talk to during this time of my life was a true blessing. It was good therapy sharing the things with her that I was going through. During one of our conversations, I came to a sad realization about how my life would have gone if I had not separated from my husband.

The conversation began when Gail said, "It looks like you've lost a few pounds since the last time I saw you."

"Yes, I have. Now that I can choose what and when I eat, I am able to make healthier choices. When Donny and I reached the point where we went to the bars a lot for dinner, we developed an unhealthy routine of eating fatty meals late at night. It caused me to put on some extra pounds, which did nothing for my figure."

After saying that, I came to a sudden realization about my life. After thinking about it for a few moments, I looked at Gail and said: "I just thought about something. What I was doing with Donny is the same exact thing that Mom was doing with Dad, and I did not even realize it until this moment. During the 30 years before I met Donny, I never drank anything with alcohol in it. Yet near the end of our marriage, I often had two or three glasses of wine with my meal when we ate at the bar late at night. And it was only because it temporarily took away the sadness that I was feeling."

After coming to this realization, I became emotional and broke down crying. I continued with what I had to say once I regained my composure.

"What was happening to me during that time is exactly what happened to Mom! She drank because Dad made her go to the bars with him. And because she was unhappy, her drinking continued to the point where it became an addiction for her. Thank God I was able to change that pattern in my life!"

I did not understand the concept of how patterns repeat themselves in our lives, and how we can change them, until Gail and I had the opportunity to listen to Gregg Braden during a Hay House event. During his presentation he talked about his book—*Fractal Time, The Secret of 2012 and a New World Age.* The book is about nature's patterns (fractals) and what they have to do with the year 2012. To explain it better, this is a quote from the inside flap of his book cover—*Applying fractal time to the history of the world and life, he proposes that everything from the war and peace between nations to the patterns of human relationships, mirror the returning cycles of our pasts. As each cycle repeats, it carries a more powerful, amplified version of itself.*

Listening to Gregg during this presentation made me think long and hard about the cycles in my own life and how they were repeated. After growing up with a father who loved alcohol, the same cycle repeated itself when I married a man who loved alcohol. The statement that I remember the most from Gregg's presentation was when he said, "The good news for everyone is that toward the end of each cycle, there is a window of opportunity to change the pattern so that it will not repeat itself at the beginning of the next cycle."

To this day and forever more, I am forever grateful and thank God that I was able to change the pattern of my life. By having the courage to end my marriage to a man who loved alcohol, I created a brand new cycle in my life, giving me the chance to find peace and happiness above and beyond anything that I could have ever imagined possible—a perfect example of Gregg's analogy.

When I drove Gail, Valerie, and Joey to the cruise ship, another beautiful feeling came over me. It was similar to what I felt on the cruise ship while listening to the piano music. After my sister and her family walked away from my car with their luggage, I glanced up at the ship. As I looked at the passengers who were already on board and waving to the traffic going by, I wished that I was one of them. At that moment, I felt mesmerized as a beautiful sensation came over me. It was a distinct feeling of knowing that I would one day be going on that exact ship with a new man—someone special whom I had not met before.

(Chapter 13)

A FEW WEEKS AFTER MY SISTER Gail left for Maryland, Tracy and I took Hazel's advice and signed up for dance lessons. Since Tracy was new to ballroom dancing, we agreed on a waltz class for beginners. Even though I already knew how to waltz, I thought it would be good to go over the basics. The class was held at the same place where I took belly dancing lessons with Tambil—the Eau Gallie Civic Center. Our first lesson was scheduled for Tuesday night with an instructor by the name of Don Wilson. When we first walked into the classroom, the only person in the room was a tall elderly gentleman we soon learned was the instructor. A few minutes later, he was joined by his assistant whose name was Candie Fowler. A graceful dancer, she was Don's perfect dance partner. When we watched them perform a remarkable dance demonstration before our class began, it was quite impressive, providing sufficient inspiration for the students to want to learn the moves that they were executing. Even though our instructor appeared to be in his later years of life, it was quite deceiving when I danced with him during the class. He had a strong frame with a stable upper body, and from the way that he interacted with me while we were dancing, it was evident that he was quite the ladies' man. The other students in the class were regulars and enjoyed helping Tracy and me with our lesson.

After our third dance class was over, Tracy informed me that she did not plan on taking the fourth and final lesson. "I hate to tell you this, Lisa, but I refuse to go back for our last dance lesson. I felt uncomfortable being around one of the students who showed up for class last night, and I won't enjoy the next class if he shows up again. I'm sorry about this."

"Don't worry about it, Tracy. If you don't feel like going, there's a dance at a place called Tropical Haven we can go to on Sunday night. One of the other students told me about it. They said it was a good place to meet other dancers who like ballroom."

"That sounds like a good idea. I'll meet you there on Sunday."

The Sunday night dance was an amazing experience and opened up a whole new world for me as far as dancing. When we arrived at the dance, we were in awe as we observed several experienced dancers gliding across a huge wooden dance floor, dancing in unison to the beat of music from the 1940s. Some of the women were wearing beautiful gowns with long, flowing skirts, and dance shoes with sequins that sparkled like diamonds. It was a sight to behold and something we never knew existed such a short distance from where we lived. Our dance instructor, Don Wilson, was running the dance, standing at the far side of the room, playing a lot of my favorite songs. As I took it all in, I thought to myself: What a wonderful place this would be if I only had a dance partner to share it all with.

During the course of the evening, we were given the opportunity to meet several men during a special dance—appropriately called a "mixer." The women lined up single file on one side of the dance floor, while the men lined up on the other side. One at a time, each man took the woman at the front of the line and danced around the room with her. When he finished dancing with her, he dropped her off at the back of the line and proceeded to the front to dance with the next woman in line. Some of the men were excellent dancers and were nice to talk to, while others were not as nice and stepped on our feet a few times. After being there for a few hours with no potential dance partners who could sweep us off our feet, Tracy and I decided it was time to leave and go home. When I sat down to remove my dance shoes, I noticed a man with silver hair and white sneakers who had just entered the dance hall. I decided to stay a while longer when

I noticed what a good dancer he was. I asked the woman sitting next to me who he was. She told me he was a dance instructor and had his own class at a different location, but she did not know exactly where.

Curious about where his class was, I decided to introduce myself to him. "Hi. My name is Lisa from Cocoa Beach."

"It's nice to meet you, Lisa. My name is Bob Kane."

"It's nice to meet you too. I was just told that you have a dance class somewhere in the local area. I just took a few classes with a girlfriend and we're looking for more classes to attend."

"That is true. My business partner and I have a place close to Cocoa Beach, and our next class is this Tuesday night. If you're interested in going, we are located in the building directly behind the mall on Merritt Island. The class starts at seven o'clock."

"Thanks for the information. I may try it out either this week or next week."

The following Tuesday was supposed to be the fourth and final lesson of the waltz class. Since Tracy stayed with her decision not to go, and I did not want to go alone, I decided instead to try the dance class closer to where I lived. I invited my friend Maria to go with me. A tall brunette in her 60s, she was someone I had met just the month before. Since she was also recently separated from her husband, another friend of mine introduced her to me. The building was easy to find since it was located right behind our favorite shopping mall on Merritt Island. As soon as Maria and I walked into the building, we noticed several displays in the hallway which looked like school projects.

When I asked the woman who was working there what the displays were all about, she told us: "During the day there are children in the building and those are their projects. The organization who works with these children is called the KLD Youth Foundation."

"That's very interesting. What is it that they do with the children?"

"They work with children who do not do well in the public school system. By providing them with a safe place to gather, and a good education based on Christian teachings, it helps them to build character and gain self-esteem."

"That's wonderful to hear. It's good to know that we're in a building where good things are happening and children are being helped. Thank you for sharing that with us. Speaking of being helped, could you tell us how to find the dance class in this building?"

"Yes. You need to go right down the hallway through those double doors."

After I thanked her, we continued down a short hallway and entered the dance area of the building. When we walked into the room, we noticed the students who were already warming up on the dance floor. The steps they were doing looked pretty interesting. And the wooden dance floor was much larger than any I had ever seen. The moment we approached the registration area to sign up for the class, my attentions were drawn to a man sitting at a nearby table. He was handsome, in a boyish sort of way, with dirty blonde hair and hazel eyes. When the instructor announced that the class was about to begin, I kept turning my head to look back at the handsome guy as I walked onto the dance floor. The class began with the women on one side of the room and the men on the other. The teacher's name was Jerry Morrison. He introduced himself as a visiting instructor from Alaska who came to Florida to share his expertise in East Coast and West Coast Swing. After he taught us a few steps, and he thought we were ready to perform them on our own, he instructed us to choose a partner to practice with. Although I was disappointed with the man who chose me, I was happy to learn that we would be changing partners every few minutes. Because I was a new woman at the dance class, each man that I met was eager to learn who I was and wanted to know everything about me.

As we moved through the rotation process, I had an opportunity to dance with the man that caught my attentions earlier. When he took me in his arms to dance, I could tell that he was an excellent dancer. After dancing with him for a few minutes, we introduced ourselves to each other. He told me his name was Alex, and then commented on my dancing when he said, "It appears that you have danced before."

"Yes, I have. A few years back, I took ballroom dance classes for two years. And just two weeks ago I took a few more, which is the reason why I'm here today. I would like to learn more."

"Since you seem to enjoy dancing so much, you may be interested to know that there's a dance party in this building next Saturday night. I think you'd have a great time if you decided to go to it."

"Thanks for letting me know. I'm sure my friend Maria will want to go with me. It will give us a chance to practice what we learn tonight."

Each time that I danced with Alex, I found myself smiling a little more. Whenever he came around in the rotation, I showed my enthusiasm by scooting across the floor to meet him. He seemed a little bashful each time that I smiled at him and excitedly greeted him with, "Hi, Alex!" When the class was almost over, I was saddened that I may not see him again.

Hoping that he would be returning for more classes, I asked him, "Are you planning on taking any more of these dance classes?"

I was pleasantly surprised by his subtle response when he said, "Yes. I signed up for all of them."

"This looks like fun. I think I will too."

After a few seconds, he looked into my eyes and told me in a relaxed tone of voice, "I'd appreciate that."

The way that he said it made me feel good. He appeared to be a perfect gentleman with a calm disposition—something I was not used to. Besides being handsome, he was extremely soft spoken and sure of himself. Looking at the muscles in his arms, I could also tell that he was athletic. When Maria and I were leaving the building, we looked for his name on the class roster to find out what his last name was. The only thing he had written on the roster was, "Alex." I went to bed that night thinking about going to the dance party on Saturday night.

The following morning, I was quite surprised when Donny came by my house and banged on my front door. When I opened the door to let him in, it was obvious he was extremely upset about something. I suspected it had something to do with his brother Bobby who had been in the hospital for several weeks. He had a serious problem with his blood pressure and the doctors could not diagnose what was causing it. As he stood in the doorway, looking as if he had been crying, I asked him, "What is the matter? Are you okay?"

Struggling with his words, he said, "No. I'm not . . . I just got back from the hospital . . . and now I have to go see my mother and tell her that Bobby isn't coming home. I can't do this alone. Would you come with me?"

Surprised that he was reaching out to me for help, I held him as he cried on my shoulder. Feeling his pain, I said, "Of course I'll go with you. I know how hard this must be for you."

On Friday night, the family had a memorial service for Bobby at the Cocoa Beach Funeral Home. To celebrate his life, Donna and her family did a wonderful job of creating a beautiful display of photos and a slide show. Out of the four brothers that he had, Bobby was always my favorite. A wonderful family man, he had such a kind nature about him. There were many people at the service who spoke very highly of him when they stood at the podium. When the service was over, Donny took me home and walked me to the back door in the garage.

As we stood in the doorway to say goodnight, I looked up at him with tears in my eyes. And then I asked him a question that had been on my mind since the day he moved out. "I know this may be a bad time to bring it up, but I need to know something. Are we ever going to talk about what went wrong with our marriage and how we can fix it?"

After saying that to him, he was silent for a few moments. And then he looked at me and said, "I don't think I ever want to talk about it. I just want to be alone."

At that moment in time, as I stood in the doorway between the garage and the house—between hanging on and letting go— something came over me that gave me the strength to say the words that I needed to say. As I looked up at him, I quietly said, "I still love you—but I realize that real love is about the other person's happiness being more important than your own. If setting you free is what will make you happy, then I will let you go."

He just cried and walked away, without saying a word. That was the moment when I finally let go. What is said about God closing one door and opening another is absolutely true, which I was about to find out the very next day.

---------------(**Chapter 14**)---------------

BOBBY'S FUNERAL SERVICE TOOK PLACE the following morning. I accompanied Donny to the funeral and made a short appearance at his mother's house afterward. When I returned to the house, I had to make preparations for a birthday party that afternoon for my friend Bonnie. Several weeks prior, I offered my home as a place to celebrate her birthday, not knowing at the time that I would be attending a funeral that morning. I thought about cancelling the party, but decided not to. I did not want to disappoint her after all the hard work that she put into planning it. When it turned out to be a cheerful afternoon, I was happy that I kept the party on my schedule. The party was a welcome change from the sadness that I felt during the days leading up to it. It was also a nice change from my previous parties at the house. Everyone who attended had a great time, and they did it without consuming a lot of alcohol. With a shuttle launch scheduled that day, it added even more to the festive atmosphere. After we watched the countdown on the television inside my living room, everyone stepped outside for a live view. It was quite spectacular watching the shuttle soar through the clouds, leaving a trail of white smoke behind it, making a thunderous crackling sound that rattled the windows in my house.

The party started winding down around seven o'clock. About that time, my friend Maria called to remind me about the Saturday night dance and to ask me what time she should pick me up. Thrilled about going to the dance, which I had on my mind the entire day, I said, "Yes! We are definitely still going to the dance tonight. It looks like the party is winding down and should be over by the time you get here."

After I hung up the phone, several people at the party mentioned that I had a sparkle in my eye, and asked me if I had a hot date for the evening. I told them that I just might have one. At the same time, I was thinking about Alex, hoping that I could see him again.

When we arrived at the dance, the room was already filled with several dancers on the floor, waltzing around the room to beautiful music. After Maria and I found a few empty chairs to sit in when we weren't dancing, we walked over to where the refreshments were. As we were walking back to our seats with a few cookies and some punch, we noticed Alex, who was sitting at a table with a few other people. When we came close to his table, I was pleasantly surprised when he immediately stood up, shook my hand, and thanked me for coming to the dance. I was utterly amazed at what a perfect gentleman he was. Because he was sitting with a few other women, I wasn't sure if he would be free to ask me to dance or not. Even if he wasn't, it was still nice seeing him again.

While sitting in our seats enjoying our snacks, I thought about what it was like as a young girl in school when we had dances in the gym—the girls on one side of the room, the boys on the other. During these events, the girls were told to sit down and wait until one of the boys asked them to dance. I always had one particular boy in mind, and sat there secretly wishing that he would pick me. After sitting with Maria for a while and thinking these thoughts, I glanced over to the part of the room where Alex was sitting. When I spotted him, I felt as if I had been transported back in time to my school days—and the boy I had secretly been thinking of was heading in my direction. Alex had left his table and was walking toward our side of the dance hall—looking straight at me.

Continuing over to where I was sitting, he offered me his hand and asked me, "Would you like to dance?"

Looking up at him with a huge smile on my face, I happily responded, "Yes! I would love to dance."

With that being said, we danced together, not only for that dance but for several more. Feeling overjoyed and filled with happiness, I thought to myself: I have found a dance partner. And he is wonderful!

During one of our dances he asked me, "What is it that you do in Cocoa Beach?"

Hesitant in telling him that I was retired from the government—sensing that he may think I was too old for him—I waited a few moments before answering him. "I used to be a secretary, and worked for the Air Force as a government employee. With a stroke of good luck, I was offered an early retirement package."

"Wow! You look way too young to me to be retired. They must have given you a pretty good deal."

"Thanks for the compliment. I love hearing that. People have been telling me that ever since I was a little girl. It used to bother me back then, but now I absolutely love it! What do you do for a living?"

"I'm a scientist working at Patrick Air Force Base."

"Wow! That is exciting. I wanted to be a scientist when I was growing up, but my father had other ideas and I became a secretary."

We talked for a while and I told him about my father dancing with Ginger Rogers while he was in the military. When I spoke about my mother, and talked about the man she dated before she met my father, his response to me was intriguing. It made me wonder what his intentions were.

"That's interesting about your mother. She must have really enjoyed her time with him. I'm really enjoying my time with you—not as if we're dating or anything."

We discovered during our conversation that his boss was someone I knew because I used to work with his wife. I could not wait to call her the next day and find out more about him. As Maria and I were preparing to leave, we told Alex we were making a stop at the video arcade on the way home. Maria suggested that I ask him to meet us there.

"Alex, would you like to follow us to the arcade and check it out?"

Thinking it was something that may not interest him; I was surprised at his response.

"Sure, I've never been to one of those before. I may as well try it."

That was the moment when I realized he definitely had a romantic interest in me—he just did not seem like the arcade type to me. When we arrived at the arcade, he was not interested in playing any of the machines. He was happy and content with just watching me play. With him sitting right next to me, I lost all interest in the machine that I was playing, thinking to myself: I wish so much that I was single, and not just separated.

As he sat there smiling at me, I told him, "There's something that I need to tell you. I'm still married, but I'm separated from my husband."

"I'm sorry. I hope he wasn't mean to you or anything."

"He was good to me for many years. And then he changed when he began drinking a lot. He moved out of the house a few months ago in February. It was very sad, but I honestly feel that there is something better out there for me."

After looking me in the eyes for a few seconds, he quietly said, "Yes, I agree—there is."

Upon hearing those words, a feeling of calmness came over me. Feeling the pain of my broken heart slowly melting away, I was thinking that he was possibly the "something better" that I was looking for. Before we left the arcade, Maria and I invited Alex to accompany us to the dance at Tropical Haven the following day. On the way home, he followed us to my house so that he would know where to pick us up for the dance on Sunday. He was thrilled when he discovered that my house was less than two miles from where he lived in Cape Canaveral. I found it unbelievable that I had met such a nice man—and he lived right in my own neighborhood.

Even though I had good vibes about Alex, Maria insisted on being a chaperone and rode with us to the Sunday night dance. We had a wonderful time that evening, and danced the night away. As I looked around the dance hall, I noticed that the dance instructor from my class with Tracy was there, as well as the teacher from the dance class where I met Alex. Seeing them together made me realize just how lucky I was to have chosen to take their classes, which led me to the moment where I met Alex. I thought about how amazing it was that we can sometimes change our lives for the better, or for the worse, simply by the choices that we make.

A funny thing happened during the Sunday night dance. Since I was in the process of having dental work done, I wore temporary teeth (referred to as a flipper) during the day until my permanent teeth were ready. Being excited about going dancing that night, I had forgotten to put in my flipper before we left the house. Although I am often told that I have a beautiful smile, it wasn't quite as beautiful that evening with two of my front teeth missing. I didn't say anything about it to Alex the entire night, hoping he would not notice.

When I did mention it to him a few days later, he let me know what his thoughts were that evening by telling me, "I could have sworn she had all her teeth when I first met her."

What made me feel really special was that he wanted to see me again, even though he thought that I was missing two front teeth. The next time that I saw Alex was on Tuesday night when he picked me up for dance class. When he arrived at my house, he presented me with a music CD.

"Hi, Lisa. I have a gift for you. I downloaded some of my favorite songs to share with you."

"Thank you! Do we have time to listen to some of them before we leave for dance class?"

"Of course we have time. Where is your CD player?"

As the first song began playing, he had a beautiful smile on his face as he waited for my response. I gave him a huge smile when I heard *Do You Wanna Dance?* by Bette Midler.

After listening to a couple more of his favorite songs, all of them having to do with love and dancing, I almost broke into tears

159

of happiness. "Thank you, Alex. This gift is something I'll always treasure. Your taste in music is exactly like mine."

Looking at me with a smile on his face, he said, "That's good!"

For the next few weeks, he continued to pick me up twice a week for dance class and was always the perfect gentleman. Riding in his car to the dance classes presented the perfect opportunity for us to talk and learn more about each other. I was shocked when he told me he had been a bachelor his entire life. How in the world such a handsome gentleman could remain a bachelor for as long as he did, was far beyond my comprehension. Adding to what he already said on the topic, he talked about his Uncle Ted who was over ninety years old and still a bachelor. He told me that his uncle inspired him to take up dancing as a way to meet women.

I also learned that he had just moved to Florida only a few weeks before I met him. He was on a special assignment to the Air Force, and his primary job was with the Las Alamos National Laboratories in New Mexico. Thinking about how close New Mexico is to Arizona—being right next to it—a funny feeling came over me. I thought about what John Rogers had told me during my reading when I mentioned that I was planning to move to Venice Beach, Florida.

"I don't see you living there. You'll most likely settle somewhere out west near the state of Arizona."

I immediately had to ask Alex, "Do you think that you'll ever move back to New Mexico?"

"Probably not. I sold the condo that I had there. I'm hoping to retire when my assignment is over. My plans are to stay here in Florida."

"Well, it may seem a little strange when I tell you this, but someone I know told me recently that they thought I would be moving to that part of the country and settling there."

"That's interesting."

After pulling into my driveway one night after dance class, I offered to cook dinner for him on the weekend. With a surprised look on his face, he said, "Wow! This relationship is moving very quickly. You want to cook me dinner?"

My own thoughts were that the relationship was moving very slowly. We had been seeing each other for over two weeks and he still had not kissed me. As I looked at him sitting next to me in the front seat of his car, something came over me. I leaned over to his side of the car and gave him a kiss. It felt so right to me that I kissed him again two more times. Then I bade him good night and left his car to go into my house.

The following Friday, he arrived at my house for dinner. Not knowing what to expect since I had kissed him the last time we met, I quickly suggested to him, "Alex, before I finish preparing dinner, I would love to show you my backyard. It's very pretty and I think you'll like sitting out there with me."

"Sure. That sounds like a good idea."

After giving him a short tour of the yard, we sat together in my favorite glider, looking over the pool and at the canal. I had bought the glider as a gift to myself shortly after I retired from the government, and enjoyed many hours sitting in it. I loved watching the tropical birds walking around the pool, listening to the sound of splashing water in the canal, caused by the mullet fish jumping high in the air, and seeing the manatees floating in the water, looking like tiny silver islands with their skin sparkling from the sunlight. This time it was especially nice because Alex was sitting right next to me. We talked for several minutes about many things, one of them being that he thought his mother would love to meet me.

It especially touched my heart when he said, "You are going to complicate my life, but in a good way. My life could use a little complicating right now."

That was the moment when I realized something magical was happening between us and he would be around for a long time. Dating someone who was such a gentleman, and did not feel the need to drink all the time, was such a pleasant change for me. When we walked together through downtown Cocoa Beach for the first time, I realized how much I had grown emotionally. Walking with him past the bars that my husband and I used to visit, I noticed my feelings of sadness had completely dissipated. They had been replaced with new feelings of happiness and gratitude. It was absolutely wonderful—almost too good to be true! With this new state of mind, I saw everything from a new perspective, as if I lived in a completely different town than I lived in before. It made me realize how true it is that although we have no control over what happens to us in life, we always have control over our attitude and how we react to it. Meeting Alex was a wonderful thing in my life, and inspired me to develop a better attitude about everything around me. I was beginning to think that my meeting him had something to do with the gift my mother had spoken of through Gordon's message, as well as the man Hazel had mentioned whom I would be unbelievably happy with. There was one thing though that I was certain was true: He most definitely did sweep me off my feet on the dance floor.

My emotional and spiritual growth was making a huge difference in how I was looking at life around me. I had learned another important lesson—just changing your thought process to something more positive and being around nicer people can also make a huge difference in your life. Almost everywhere that I went with Alex, we ran into people that I knew. Each time it happened, they commented on how much better I looked and how happy I was. Some of my friends, whom I had not seen for a while, did not even recognize me. The transformation I had gone through was nothing short of miraculous, both physically and emotionally.

As our relationship grew in the coming weeks, I began sharing some of my spiritual beliefs and experiences with him. He referred to them as "magical moments," telling me, "I can certainly understand why you believe, but I would like to have my own experiences before I can believe." Realizing that he had a background in science, I understood why he said this. The good part was that even though he did not have some of the same beliefs that I had, it was easy for me to share my thoughts and beliefs with him.

The first magical moment that I shared was the story about what happened while I was parked in front of the Disney cruise ship, shortly after my sister Gail and her family walked away with their luggage.

"Alex, when I looked up at that ship, such a beautiful feeling came over me. I had a feeling of knowing that someday I would go on that same ship with a new man in my life."

I was pleasantly surprised when he said, "Gee, I wonder who that person could be?"

He was so receptive to my sharing the experience with him that I felt comfortable telling him about the message I received from my mother.

"Alex, I would love to share another story with you. It is something I experienced while on a cruise with my older sister Gail."

"Would this experience be another one of your magical moments?"

"Yes. You could definitely call it that. Before I tell you what happened on the cruise, I need to first tell you what happened the last time that I saw my mother. Twenty-four years ago, just hours before she died, I was sitting next to her hospital bed and holding her hand. Even though she was in a coma, and the nurse told me she could not speak, she did."

"That's interesting. What magical thing did she say?"

"She told me she did not know what to do . . . if she should stay here or go there. Thinking that there was an angel talking to her, I told her to go to Heaven because I thought she would be happier."

"Wow . . . that certainly is another magical moment for you."

"Well, that's not the whole story; I have more to tell you. For the next twenty-four years, I cried each time that I told anyone about the last time I saw my mother. All that changed when I received a message from her during a cruise that I took with my sister Gail. Since I received the message, I don't cry anymore when I talk about my mother."

"That's interesting. I would love to hear what happened on your cruise."

"On the last night of the cruise, I spoke to my mother out loud in my cabin and told her that I would love to hear from her. When I later joined my sister in the auditorium for the last seminar of the cruise, there was a man on the stage whose name was Gordon Smith. I was shocked when he gave me a message from my mother. As part of the message, he told me that she was giving me a gift from Heaven that would be eternal and lasting. I have been trying for months to figure out the meaning of her message as it pertains to the gift."

Not knowing how he would react to my own thoughts about the message, I paused for a moment before continuing. He was either going to think I was crazy, stop seeing me, or just maybe my intuitions were correct and he would understand how I felt.

"Alex . . . I honestly feel with all my heart that my meeting you may have something to do with the gift from my mother."

As I patiently waited for his response, I briefly remembered how crushed I was after I shared the same story with my ex-husband several months before.

After several seconds of silence, he finally responded to what I had told him. "Gee, that's an awful lot to live up to."

I did not mention anything more about my magical moments until the following day, and then I asked him what his thoughts were on the stories that I shared with him. He gave me the most wonderful answer.

"I love listening to all your stories, Lisa. And I completely understand why you believe. If those things happened to me, I would believe too."

The following weekend, he invited me to his townhouse near the beach so that he could cook me dinner. A beautiful place, it was only steps away from a wooden walkway that reached over the sand dunes onto a beautiful sandy beach. It was a perfect spot to watch the cruise ships as they were leaving the port and the rocket launches from Cape Canaveral Air Force Station. The grounds around his townhouse were beautifully landscaped with tropical plants and a gorgeous bird of paradise on the left as I walked down the sidewalk toward the front entrance. Stepping through the front doorway, I entered a foyer with a large kitchen in front of me and the living room to the right. To the left of the kitchen, I saw double doors which opened to the downstairs guest suite. There were several framed prints of mermaids on the walls which caught my eye. Upstairs there were two more bedrooms.

The first bedroom was a master suite with a balcony that overlooked the ocean and the tennis courts. The second bedroom was another guest suite with a private path. In between the two bedrooms was a loft that he used as an office. It was like being in a library. There were shelves and shelves of books on various mathematical and science topics.

I asked him, "If I were to read all these books, would I be as smart as you are?"

I was surprised when he said, "If you read all these books, you would be smarter than me."

Even though his home had the look of a bachelor pad, with exercise equipment in the living room, I felt comfortable being there. After we ate dinner, we enjoyed a romantic evening and snuggled up to each other on the sofa as we watched a movie. Other evenings when I visited him, we played a lot of *Scrabble* games, which he normally won. He was a competitive player but I did manage to beat him on a few occasions. Lucky for me, most of the scientific words that he knew required more than the seven letters that were available for each player to form words.

The following week, he came by my house and we had a discussion about our first trip together. While we were sitting in front of my computer and surfing the internet, he asked me, "Do you have any plans yet for the Fourth of July weekend?"

"No, I don't have any plans. Why do you ask?"

"My brother and sister want me to meet them in Pennsylvania that week, but it's for a sad occasion. My mother's health is not good and it may be the last time that we'll see her. The trip would be a lot nicer if you could come with me."

"I would love to go with you, Alex, and I look forward to meeting your family."

"Great! I'll make some plane reservations."

Toward the end of June, his mother's health took a turn for the worse and he had to change his flight to visit her a few days early. He told me not to change my flight reservations and to meet up with him on the date we originally planned. He was able to spend several days with his mother before she passed, and visited with her for hours at a time each day, just holding her hand and sitting with her.

By the time I arrived in Pennsylvania, it was only one day before her funeral service. Instead of meeting just his brother Steve and his sister Paula, I met every single member of his family, in addition to several close friends. Having done most of their crying during the days leading up to the funeral, by the time I arrived, they were focused on celebrating her life. Every person I met made me feel right at home, and I almost felt like a member of the family. Since I did not know his mother, and everyone had such a pleasant disposition, I almost forgot the real reason why we were there. His family was simply amazing and pleasant to be around.

When I woke up the morning of the funeral and encountered his brother, Steve, in the hallway, he greeted me by saying, "Good morning, Lisa. How are you feeling today?"

Completely forgetting that he was preparing for his mother's funeral, and thinking about how happy I was to be spending time with his brother Alex, I responded with, "I am unbelievably happy! How are you today, Steve?"

I did not realize what I said was inappropriate until Alex reminded me that his brother had just gotten dressed to go to their mother's funeral when I said it. Since it was an innocent mistake on my part, he did not become upset with me and even thought it was a little humorous. When I walked down the stairs to have breakfast, there was music coming from the stereo in the living room and I could have sworn that I heard the *Wedding March* which is played for the recessional when the bride and groom exit the ceremony. I mentioned it to a few people but no one else heard it.

We went to the funeral service that day and everyone paid their respects to a woman who was obviously well-loved and respected in the community. Since his mother requested a Catholic Ukrainian mass, it was extremely long. Throughout the entire mass, I heard a cantor in the back of the church chanting psalms from the Old Testament. Listening to him, and smelling the incense that the priest used during the service, I envisioned being in a scene from the movie

The Godfather. On the altar there were sliding gates which were opened during the mass to symbolize opening the gates to Heaven for the departed. Near the end of the funeral service, the priest invited everyone to say their farewells to his mother. She was in an open casket in front of the altar. The exact moment that Alex and I walked up to her casket to say our farewells, an elderly gentleman approached us and asked Alex, "Is this lovely woman your wife?"

The following morning, Alex and I went to breakfast at the Cracker Barrel. Every time that I have gone to this restaurant, I always admired the antiques and old photographs that are part of their décor. After they sat us at our table, we ordered our breakfast. I then noticed something odd about the antique décor display on the wall next to our table. There were several black-and-white photographs of wedding couples from the early nineteen hundreds.

I had to ask Alex, "Did your mother want you to get married?"

"Yes, she did, but I think she gave up on me."

"Well, I don't think she's given up on you yet. Look at the photographs on the wall next to our table. They are pictures of weddings. I think she's been sending me messages and this is the third one that I've noticed. This morning I heard the *Wedding March* when I walked into your sister Paula's living room. It was coming from her stereo. Why would any radio station play that song just out of the blue? And during the funeral, someone asked you if I was your wife. It was the exact moment that we walked up to your mother's casket."

"That's interesting, Lisa. It does sound like a strange coincidence."

When we returned home from Pennsylvania, I received a fourth message which I believe was from his mother. It happened while I was having my nails done at the local Tips and Toes salon in Cocoa Beach. While I was sitting with my friend, Linh, who was doing my nails, her little sister was sitting down in front of a keyboard practicing her piano lessons. Excited about my recent trip to Pennsylvania, I began telling her about it as she worked on my nails.

"I just returned from Pennsylvania with Alex and had a wonderful time. Even though the purpose of the trip was to attend his mother's funeral, everyone in his family was extremely nice to me and made me feel right at home."

"I'm sorry to hear about his mother. What was her name?"

"Her name was Mary."

Just seconds after I mentioned her name, a young man sat down at the keyboard and began playing a song which gave me goose bumps when I heard it.

"Oh my God! Someone is at the keyboard and he is playing the *Wedding March*. It's so odd that he is playing that song because I just mentioned Mary's name. I think she's sending me another message that she wants me to marry her son."

"Wow! If she is, I think you should marry him. He sounds like a really nice guy."

─────(Chapter 15)─────

A WEEK LATER, I HAD TO leave Alex for eight days for a trip to Massachusetts. Before I met him, I had planned a trip with Donny's mother, Lorraine, to visit our friends Joe and Jean in Westport, Massachusetts. They lived in a gorgeous house built near a wooded area, several miles from the closest town. Each morning during my visit, I was awakened by the sweet sound of birds chirping outside my bedroom window. Perched in the trees in the backyard, they were eating food from the bird feeders which Joe carefully hung on the branches each morning. I was in seventh heaven when I sat on their back porch each day, taking pictures of yellow finches, blue jays, cardinals, and hummingbirds. The hummingbirds moved so quickly that it took several photo shoots to capture them. When I did, I was fascinated with the photos.

Right after breakfast each morning, Joe and I took a two-mile walk around the block. During this journey, we walked past several farms, went through the woods by way of gravel roads, observed the swans swimming in the lake, and occasionally stopped to talk to the two women who were walking their pet llamas. The ladies who owned the llamas were friends of Joe and Jean and their names were Nancy and Joanne. When I first saw them, I had to ask, "Is it OK if I pet the llamas? They are so adorable!"

Nancy quickly answered me and said, "Of course you can. They have a very gentle nature."

"It's interesting that you have them as pets and you can walk them with a leash. Can you tell me more about them?"

"Oh yes. We love to talk about them. We originally got them to help us with our yard work. Since they graze on our land, we don't have to mow the grass anymore. And we use their droppings as fertilizer for our vegetable gardens and flowerbeds. Llama droppings are actually the best fertilizer there is. Unlike other fertilizers, it can be used fresh or dry and does not need to be supplemented with things like nitrogen, phosphorous, or potassium. And it makes our vegetables and edible flowers taste a lot better."

"That's really interesting. I have heard about edible flowers. Is it true that high-end chefs use them as garnishes on their entrees?"

"Yes, they do. And the flowers are also used to decorate wedding cakes."

"Wedding cakes . . ." I murmured.

Joe and Jean had many interesting friends who lived in their neighborhood. I had the pleasure of meeting their friend Anna when she invited us to her home for a glass of fresh-squeezed lemonade. When we arrived at the entrance to her long driveway, I noticed the natural rock wall and the small containers of flowers which she put by the road for potential customers. Her beautiful wooden house was surrounded by several acres of land filled with trees, gardens, and bushes with flowers. I took a stroll through her gardens and took several photographs of her flowers. We had a lovely time hearing about the farm that she lived on and the many adventures with her children. She was extremely proud of one of her sons who was on his way to becoming a professional golfer. When I took a walk one morning on my own, I took a wrong turn and got lost. After walking down several streets in the neighborhood, I recognized Anna's beautiful home and paid her another visit. I was thrilled when she offered me some of her homemade brownies with walnuts on top.

When we drove to the closest town, the landscape was similar to what I remembered when I had visited my brother Daniel in England years before. Just like the English countryside, the homes in Westport had several acres of grass-covered land that were bordered by rock walls, some of them natural and some of them manmade. Many of the homes in her town were located on property that was previously used for farming. To keep the area from being overdeveloped, only one house was allowed to be built on each piece of property, regardless of how many acres of land it had.

We had a wonderful time during our visit, going to dinner, visiting friends, playing lots of card games, and going to the beach. Since I had not yet told Lorraine about Alex, not knowing how she would feel about me dating someone, I had to be quiet while I talked to him on the phone each day. I was, however, able to share the news of my newfound love with Joe and Jean, and told them how unbelievably happy I was. They were happy for me, and also understood why I had recently separated from my husband.

When I returned from the trip, I immediately went to see Alex. I missed him terribly after being away from him for over a week. Seconds after he opened the front door to let me into his house, he embraced me with a huge hug and then kissed me.

"Welcome back home, Lisa. I have something special for you."

Looking past his shoulder at his kitchen countertop, I noticed a vase of gorgeous, long-stemmed red roses. There was also a box of chocolates sitting right next to the roses. I immediately had a strange feeling come over me, thinking about something John Rogers had said about roses during my reading with him.

"Your husband will try to win you back. I see him giving you red roses."

Thinking about that for a moment, I realized something. If I had not changed my life by choosing a new path to follow—a path which led me to Alex—the same red roses could have come from Donny. Still being available to him, he eventually could have persuaded me to go back to him once he realized what he had lost. Then I would have been in the same situation as before, married to a man who would never stop drinking. I firmly believe that having the courage to choose a new path in my life caused the red roses to be from someone else. I thanked God at that moment that the red roses were from Alex.

When I asked him a few months later why he had not bought me any more flowers, he gave me a puzzled look and said, "I normally don't ever buy flowers."

Then I had to ask him, "Well, why did you buy me red roses when I came back from my trip to Massachusetts?"

"I don't really know why. It just happened."

In order to be fair to Alex, I focused more on finishing the paperwork for my divorce. Using my secretarial skills and good common sense, I educated myself on the process and completed the paperwork within a few weeks. I then hired an attorney to review it to ensure that it went through the courts as quickly as possible. When I presented the papers to my husband for his signature, he signed them without even reading them, trusting that I had his best interest at heart when I prepared them. It was an exciting day for me when I drove to the courthouse to file my divorce papers. Since my friend Tracy worked at the courthouse, she helped me to make sure everything was in order when I arrived. My papers were filed the first week of July and I was given a court date of August 8, 2008. I found it interesting that the numbers for my court date were all eights, the number which symbolizes new births or new beginnings. Many Christians even believe that the number eight symbolizes the resurrection.

With my birthday only a few weeks away, I began making plans for my birthday party. For the past several years, I celebrated my birthday with the spirit of Christmas in mind, and called it the "Annual Christmas in July Party." Each year I put up the Christmas tree, with all the decorations that went with it, and prepared a feast with many varieties of food. When our guests arrived, they received the ultimate holiday experience, as if it really was the twenty-fifth of December. For Donny and me, it had been the big event of the year at our house, with anywhere from fifty to one hundred of our friends in attendance. Since most of our friends enjoyed celebrating with alcoholic beverages, we hired a bartender for the evening. This year I decided on a much smaller celebration, and invited only my closest friends. Since I was still good friends with my mother-in-law,

Lorraine, I invited her to my party and let her know that my dancing partner would also be there. Because she understood my current situation with her son, and was curious about my "dance partner," she happily accepted my invitation.

Alex was the first to arrive at the party, followed by the rest of the guests. We kept the refreshments light by serving a few appetizers along with the usual cake and ice cream. My friend Bonnie baked a delicious chocolate cake, beautifully decorated with frosting and strawberries. My friend Rebecca Dance, who was one of my doctors, brought all the fixings to make her famous chocolate martinis. The party provided me the perfect opportunity to introduce more of my friends to Alex. When Lorraine arrived at the front door, he was standing right beside me as she walked into the house. I politely introduced them to each other, and then she walked into the living room to find a place to sit down.

A few minutes later, he asked me, "Excuse me, but who is this woman Lorraine that you just introduced me to?"

Almost too embarrassed to tell him who she was, I answered, "Oh, Lorraine . . . she's my mother-in-law."

Looking as if he was comfortable with what I said, he told me, "OK."

I noticed later on that he was sitting next to her on the living room sofa and was having a conversation with her. Watching him sitting with her made me feel really good. He was the perfect gentleman the entire evening, and everyone who met him thought he was a perfect match for me.

Later on in the evening, Lorraine approached me and said, "I really like Alex! He is handsome and he has excellent manners."

I could not help it when I responded by saying, "Unlike your son."

Hearing my response, she looked at me and said, "Oh yes."

I was pleased when she called me a few weeks later and asked me with enthusiasm, "Are you still dating Alex?" When I told her that I was, she responded with, "I'm happy for you, Lisa. It's good that you have someone so nice for companionship."

"Thank you, Lorraine. Hearing you say that makes me feel good."

Over the next few weeks, I counted the days as I waited for my day in court—the day when I would no longer be married to a man who loved alcohol. During this time, Alex and I talked about taking a short vacation once my divorce was final. Knowing that Venice Beach was my favorite place to visit, he made plans for us to go there for a few days. When he called to tell me his plan, it made me feel really special.

"Hi, Lisa. All the arrangements have been made for our trip to Venice."

"Thank you, Alex. It means so much to me that you're doing this. What day are we leaving?"

"I thought it would be nice if we left on the day of your divorce. I don't want you to be sad on that day. How about leaving right after you come home from the hearing?"

"That is a perfect idea. Thank you, Alex!"

Because he planned to leave on our trip the same day as my divorce hearing, it put me in a completely different state of mind than I would have been in otherwise—changing my focus to looking forward to a new relationship with lots of promise, rather than looking backward on a marriage that failed.

Since I chose the fastest and simplest form of divorce, Donny had to accompany me to the courthouse for the hearing. I could have driven by myself to the courthouse, but I wanted to make sure that he showed up so I insisted that he drive me there. The day started out at 7:30 a.m. when he came by the house to pick me up. As he drove me to the courthouse in his blue Chevy van, my mind was not on the divorce hearing. Instead, I was thinking about my trip later that day to Venice Beach. Filled with enthusiasm, I looked forward to being with Alex for the next few days, and I did not think about the man sitting beside me who would soon be my *ex-husband*. When we arrived at the courtroom waiting area, there were three other couples waiting for their hearings to begin. Needless to say, they did not share the same overwhelming enthusiasm that I had. When our names were announced, we entered the courtroom and stood before the judge. She asked us to raise our hands so that we could be sworn in. After answering a few simple questions, the hearing was over—taking less than five minutes. As we walked out of the courtroom, the judge complimented me on my paperwork and offered me a job at the courthouse.

I politely replied, "Thank you for your offer, but I've already served my time as a secretary and would prefer to keep my freedom."

Since my friend Tracy was working at the courthouse that day, I insisted that we stop by her office to say hello. When we arrived at the area where she worked, she was so excited to see me that she ran across the room to give me a huge hug. She also hugged Donny, but told me later on that it was difficult for her to do that. Knowing that she wasn't happy with the way he had been treating me, I could understand why she said that.

During the ride home in his van, my emotions were mixed as I thought about the sadness of what had just happened minutes before, and the happiness of what lay ahead. Furthermore, I thought about how unhappy the day would have been if Alex had not come into my life. I was extremely grateful for the new path I had followed and the choices I had made that took me down this path—feeling strongly that my choices were influenced by spiritual intervention from my mother in Heaven.

Not more than a minute after Donny dropped me off at the house, I called Alex to tell him I was home and my divorce hearing was over. Within ten minutes he arrived at my house, looking thrilled that I was finally a single woman. When we drove to Venice that day, I felt the sadness of my past melting away with each mile that took us away from Cocoa Beach. Thinking about the three days ahead of us, I looked forward to visiting my favorite beaches, going to dinner each night; and best of all, looking for the shiny black shark's teeth that wash up on the beaches.

On the first day of our trip, we went to Venice Municipal Beach. Walking distance from the historic downtown area, the beach had a boardwalk, a snack bar, and a funky wing-shaped pavilion where local musicians played on the weekend. After spending the day at the beach, we walked down tree-lined Venice Avenue toward the historic downtown area. We spent hours strolling through the many shops and art galleries. Toward the end of the day, we visited my favorite restaurant in Venice—Sharkey's on the Pier. The only beachfront restaurant in Venice, it was at the foot of a long fishing pier which reached out into the Gulf of Mexico. After dinner we walked to the end of the fishing pier and watched a spectacular sunset over the water. We completed the evening by visiting the tiki hut and danced under the stars.

The next day we took a 20-minute drive to one of the most beautiful beaches in the world—Siesta Beach. On a barrier island just off shore of Sarasota, Siesta Beach is renowned for its breathtaking sunsets, easygoing waves, and gorgeous, crystal-white sand. As we walked toward the boardwalk, the view was magnificent. We feasted our eyes on a beach with sand so white that it looked like a blanket of snow. We found it interesting when we learned that the sand is ninety-nine percent pure quartz; making it soft and cool on the feet regardless of how hot the sun is on any given day. Being a scientist, Alex was impressed with one of the many awards recognizing the quality of the sand—the 1987 Great International White Sand Challenge. For this award, the sand was scientifically proven to be the finest and whitest in the world. After walking through this wonderful sand, we picked a spot on the beach and set up a small beach tent. Sheltering us from the sun, it provided a cool place to sit and relax. When we swam in the warm waters of the gulf, the water was so clear that we could see the bottom, as if we were vacationing somewhere in the Caribbean Islands.

Later that day, we ventured out to Caspersen Beach—my absolute favorite place on planet Earth. Left in its natural state—uncultivated, windswept, and secluded—Caspersen Beach is known as the "Shark Tooth Capital of the World." A sharp contrast to Siesta Beach with its crystal-white sand, the sand at this beach is black, with several large rocks on the shoreline. A perfect natural setting, it attracts fishermen and fossil hunters from all over the world. The fossilized teeth come from a fossil bed that lies offshore, consisting of a huge deposit of fossil bones and teeth from ancient mammals and giant sharks. The combination of wave action and storms constantly washes the teeth and other fossils onto the shore. Alex helped me search for some of the fossils and then we took a rest as the sun began to set. Relaxing on a beach blanket in the black sand, we watched the sky change to a magnificent orange as the sun disappeared over the horizon.

When we saw the first star of the night, I asked him, "Is it true that you can make a wish on the first star that you see and your wish will come true?" Although I was hoping for a romantic discussion to begin, what I got was a short educational talk on how the stars are created. I should have known it would happen since one of his degrees is in astronomy.

A few months later, I decided to introduce him to my world of cruising and suggested that we take a four-day cruise on Royal Caribbean's Monarch of the Seas. After I booked the cruise, I was concerned that he may become seasick or just not enjoy the experience. Luckily, he did like cruising and we had a great time together. During the cruise, we were presented with the perfect opportunity to show off some of our dance moves. It happened during formal night when we were sitting in the auditorium for the captain's gala event. Once we were introduced to the captain of the ship and all the senior officers, the orchestra began playing dance music. While Alex and I were relaxing and listening to the music, they made an announcement inviting everyone in the audience to dance on the stage.

Eager to dance with him, I told him, "This is where we go up on the stage and do a waltz."

Looking at me with a surprised look on his face, he said, "You've got to be kidding! No one is up there right now."

"Trust me on this one. I have danced on the stage many times before on other cruises. Once one couple goes up on stage, several others always join in."

Reluctantly, he agreed to join me for a dance, looking a little uncomfortable once we were on the stage. By the time the orchestra started playing the music, we realized that no one else would be joining us and we would be the only couple on the stage. Being the proud dancer that he was and always taking his dancing seriously, he took me in his arms and glided me around the wooden stage floor, right in step to a beautiful waltz. When the dance was over, we heard a huge applause. As we squinted our eyes so that we could see through the bright spotlights that were shining on the stage, we looked out at an audience of several hundred people who were clapping for us. It was such a beautiful moment—one that I shall never forget. It was especially rewarding when one young couple approached us and told us we had inspired them to take dance classes.

The next cruise that we took was only a few months after that. I researched all the ships at the port and was able to book a fabulous cruise at a phenomenal price. It was purely by accident that it happened to be the same ship from one of my magical moment stories. It was the story where I had the beautiful feeling of going on a ship with someone new in my life. The ship was the Disney Wonder.

Since the price that I found was only good for a short time, I immediately called him on the phone and asked him, "How would you like to go on a Disney cruise for your Christmas present?"

Happily accepting my gift, we were all set for our next cruise together. As soon as we boarded the ship, they announced our names and directed us to the buffet. For our evening meals, we rotated (along with our servers) between three themed restaurants. I will never forget the time that I cruised with my sister Gail and her family on one of the Disney ships. On the second night of our cruise, her grandson Joey was not aware that the wait staff followed us each night when we changed restaurants. I could not stop laughing when he asked the waitress, "Excuse me, but why did you quit your job at that other restaurant and now you're working here?"

Even though there were thousands of children on the ship, there were plenty of areas where children were not allowed. The adult-only swimming pool was heated with fresh water and the whirlpools were absolutely wonderful. Our favorite part of the ship was the Rainforest Room. Located in the ship's spa area, it was set up for men and women to enjoy together, as long as they wore bathing suits and used the robes that were provided for them. There were heated tile beds to relax on, wet and dry saunas, and special showers with several jets spraying water. We spent many hours relaxing in that room and enjoying all that it had to offer. What I enjoyed most about the room was relaxing on the heated tile beds, feeling the warmth of the tiles, listening to soft music playing in the background—creating the perfect place for either daydreaming or reading a good book.

My favorite night of the cruise was the "Captain's Night"—an elegant evening with the ladies wearing evening gowns and the men wearing suits or tuxedos. While waiting in line to have our photograph taken with the captain, we noticed the couple in front of us being introduced as Mr. and Mrs.

I was somewhat surprised when Alex asked me, "Should we also be introduced as Mr. and Mrs.?"

"Sure. I think it would be a fun thing to do."

During the rest of the cruise, he made more subtle hints about his feelings for me, but remained noncommittal. When the ship docked in the Bahamas at Nassau, I had an opportunity to give him a not-so-subtle hint of what my feelings were for him. As we walked down Bay Street, we discovered several high-end designer stores selling designer fashions, handbags, perfume, shoes, gifts, and most important of all, jewelry. During our walk, I made certain that we went into the first large jewelry store that we saw. As soon as we entered the store, I made my way over to the jewelry counter where the diamond rings were. Alex, having something different on his mind, looked at the many different watches.

Looking at the beautiful rings in the glass case, I pointed to one that I liked, and told the salesman, "I would love to try that ring on and show it to my boyfriend."

Anticipating a possible sale, the salesman was agreeable. "Why of course, miss. There's no problem with doing that."

Wearing the ring proudly on my left hand, I yelled at Alex who was on the other side of the store—still looking at watches. "Alex! Look at this ring. Doesn't it look beautiful on my finger?"

He slowly walked across the room and glanced at it. With a blank look on his face, he just stood there and said nothing. When I turned around to give the ring back to the salesman, he commented on the situation. "I don't think he's ready for this yet. It looks like we scared him away."

When I turned around, I did not see him anywhere. After searching everywhere in the store for him, I eventually found him standing outside the front door, looking anxious, ready to move on to the next store.

When we returned from the cruise, I decided to take some of the money that I received from my divorce and do some much-needed renovations to my house. In particular, I wanted to complete all of the projects that Donny left undone. My hopes were that one day Alex and I would be married, and finishing the renovations would make it easier to sell the house. I hired a local contractor by the name of Steve Cook to do the work. Over the next several months, he did an extraordinary job updating three bedrooms, remodeling the master bath, and finishing the garage. With each job that he completed, I felt like the house took on a new personality. Once the inside of the house was finished, I had the dock repaired and had a hut built over the water. With the hut located at the end of the canal, it was the perfect place for viewing spectacular sunsets over the river.

Since I loved to entertain and have friends over for dinner, I invested in some new dining room and living room furniture. Once a month, I cooked a special dinner and Alex and I invited some of our mutual friends to join us. During one of these dinners, there was an interesting discussion about his Uncle Ted. There were six of us sitting around the dinner table when his name came up in conversation. Someone had asked Alex what inspired him to take dance classes.

"It was my uncle Ted. He loved to dance and suggested I take dance classes as a way to meet women. Would you believe that he is over ninety years old and is still a bachelor? I admire him for that and have also remained a bachelor, or at least so far I have."

After his last comment, I gave him a little smirk and said, "Oh yeah? So far you have."

Over the next several months, he remained totally noncommittal. Valentine's Day and my birthday came and went without receiving the special gift that I was wishing for—an engagement ring. Although the cards that he gave me were always romantic and signed, "Love, Alex," he never wrote the special words on the cards that my heart longed to see—"I love you." Whenever I asked him if he thought we would be together forever, he always gave me the same answer, or something similar: "I'll be around for a long time. I am not going anywhere."

For the month of September, we decided to take a longer vacation. We booked a seven-day cruise to the Eastern Caribbean on Royal Caribbean's Freedom of the Seas. His brother Steve and wife Cindi decided to go with us, which turned it into a family event. They arrived from Tyler, Texas a few days early to have some time to unwind before the cruise, spending most of that time relaxing in the sun and hanging out at the beach. The night before the cruise, the four of us attended a Toga party at The Cocoa Beach pier. Since none of us had costumes, we had to be creative by making them out of old sheets. I thought it was hilarious when Steve added a cape to his costume and told everyone at the party that he was Superman. Not as reserved as his brother, he kept us laughing the entire evening with all of his jokes.

The following morning, we loaded up the luggage in the back of my Toyota 4-Runner and drove to Port Canaveral. Everyone was overwhelmed when we boarded the ship and entered the Royal Promenade. Longer than a football field, and taking up four of the ship's fifteen decks, it was considered the heartbeat of the ship. When we strolled past the many shops, cafes, and lounges, it felt like we were walking down the main street of a town. After our stroll, we explored the rest of the ship and then ate lunch before we went to our cabins to unpack. As we reviewed the itineraries that were placed in our cabins, we looked forward to seven relaxing days at sea with a few stops at exotic islands in the Eastern Caribbean.

Our first port of call was the island of St Thomas, a beautiful tropical island with hilly terrain and pristine beaches lapped by turquoise waters. Our ship docked near the picturesque harbor town of Charlotte Amalie, known for its great, duty-free shopping. Shortly after disembarking from the ship, the four of us took a taxi ride to the downtown shopping area. As we walked through the streets, darting in and out of various shops, we enjoyed checking out all the various types of merchandise. Thinking about a store I had been to during previous visits to the island, I invited everyone to visit a jewelry store where I knew the owner by name. His name was George. I met him when one of the other power equipment dealers up north suggested Donny and I check out his store during one of our cruises. Tall, dark, and handsome, he had a gift for gab and was an excellent salesman. As soon as we walked into the store, he greeted us and offered each of us a glass of soda with a splash of Caribbean rum. When we began drinking our sodas, they tasted more like a glass of rum with a splash of soda. I suspect that the jewelry stores do this as a way of putting their customers into a shopping mood. After we took a few more sips, Cindi and I began checking out the jewelry. Not interested in looking at jewelry, Alex and his brother Steve chose to look at watches. Since I scared Alex away from the store the last time I looked at diamond rings, I decided to look at earrings instead. George showed me several gorgeous hoop earrings with diamonds in them. While I was trying them on, Alex came over to watch me as I decided on the pair that I wanted.

"I think I like these earrings, George. The diamonds have a nice sparkle to them."

"That's a great choice, Lisa. Those hoops are pretty popular right now. There are diamonds outside and inside the hoop. Will you be paying for these with a credit card?"

After I reached for my charge card and then laid it on the counter, Alex interrupted the sales transaction and reached for his wallet.

"I'll take care of paying for those."

"Thank you, Alex! That is so sweet of you. This is such a special moment—my first piece of jewelry from you!"

I gave him a huge hug and a kiss and told him that I loved him. Before we left the store, he looked at a few more watches. He did not buy a watch, but his brother found a really nice Rolex and bought it for himself. It was one that he had always wanted and the price was right. Cindi also did some shopping and bought a few pieces of jewelry for her daughters. Everyone was happy when we left the store—especially George.

When we returned to the ship, we cleaned up for dinner, which was followed by the after-dinner show. After watching a spectacular show with singing and dancing, Alex and I strolled through the promenade. When I noticed a store that specialized in Canadian diamonds, I told Alex, "Since you were born in Canada, I think we should check out the Canadian diamonds in this store." Although I succeeded in having him take a closer look than our last shopping adventure in the Bahamas, I was disappointed when he told me he'd rather look at watches.

After the cruise, it was back to our normal routine of seeing each other several times a week and continuing our many dance classes. Being together for an entire week was a great experience and strengthened our relationship. A few days after being home from our cruise, he made an interesting comment while we were driving home from one of our dance classes.

"Lisa, it was nice being with you for seven days in a row. I miss it."

Very surprised at what he said, I had to ask him, "Do you ever envision us being together every day?"

Although it sounded like he had good intentions for our relationship, his comment was still noncommittal when he said, "It looks like we're heading in that direction."

Knowing that we were heading in that direction, as he said, I tried my best to be patient with him, thinking that he would take the relationship to the next level whenever he was ready. It was obvious to me that he loved me, evidenced by how much time he spent with me and how loving and caring he was when we were together. We had several things in common and enjoyed everything that we did together. In addition to having a love for dancing and music, he also enjoyed playing my favorite board game *Scrabble*. Even better than that, he loved to go shopping with me, and I mean really shopping. Every place that we went, he strolled through the shops with me and looked at all the things that I enjoyed looking at. If we went to a kitchen store, we looked at all the kitchen gadgets. If we went into a clothing shop, he would go into the men's section while I went into the women's section. He was an unbelievable boyfriend and everything that I wanted in a man—and also a husband.

(Chapter 16)

OVER THE NEXT FEW MONTHS, we expanded on our knowledge and learned a new dance called contra dancing. The first Saturday of every month we went to the dance at the Cocoa Beach Recreation Center, and the third Friday we went to the dance in Melbourne at Tropical Haven. Having common roots with square dancing, we noticed that contra dancing had some subtle differences from the square dancing that we were familiar with. For starters, the dance is always done to live music, the band being composed of three or more musicians, and there is a caller who runs the dance by calling out each dance step the entire evening. While square dancers tend to arrive at a dance with their partners and dance exclusively with their partners, contra dancers do the same thing, with one exception. They spend most of the evening dancing with a variety of partners. Another difference we noticed is that the dance required more energy than the usual square dance, with lots of spinning and swinging your partner. Sometimes while we were dancing, I noticed men swinging their partners so fast that their feet came off the floor.

Alex and I made several new friends by going to these dances. In addition to being loads of fun, contra dancing was also a good way to stay in shape because it required a lot of energy. Most of the people we met at the contra dances, as well as other dances that we attended, always assumed that Alex and I were already married. Whenever the assumption was made, I always felt a little sad when

I had to correct them by saying, "No, we're not married. We're just dating." Sometimes Alex would tell me that someone approached him and told him the same thing. And then he would say nothing more about it. It was like torture to me, teasing me with the subject but not letting me know what his real intentions were.

With the beginning of the New Year, Alex received some bad news at work about his assignment at Patrick Air Force Base. While driving to one of our dance classes, he broke the news to me.

"Lisa, I found out today there may be a problem with renewing my assignment with the Air Force. I may have to move back to New Mexico in March. And that is only two months from now. My supervisors assumed that everything was going OK with my extension, until they discovered a ruling they overlooked that could change things."

Concerned about what would happen to our relationship, I asked him: "What will happen to us? Does this move mean that we're going to have a long-distance relationship or perhaps we'll no longer be seeing each other?"

"Well, the plan at the moment is for you to come with me."

At first I was thrilled that he wanted me to be with him in New Mexico, but then reality set in. Knowing that I still had no commitment from him, I had an uneasy feeling about his so-called "plan at the moment." All I could say to him was, "Oh, I see."

Over the next few weeks, I was torn between my thoughts of going with him or not going with him. I received more than enough advice on the situation from several of my friends and relatives. Most of them told me that I was crazy to go with him if I did not have a ring on my finger. I even received advice from some of his close relatives. They reminded me that he had lived alone for most of his life and was pretty much content with the way things were.

After thinking it through for several days, I brought it up again. "Alex, if you do end up moving back to New Mexico, I would like to go with you; however, I want you to know that I have a back-up plan. My plan is to first put my house on the market so that I can sell it.

Then, if things don't go well with us living together, I'll just move to Venice Beach, which was my original plan before I met you."

Sounding a bit surprised at this statement from me, he told me: "I don't think you should give up your house, Lisa. It's a beautiful piece of property; it's in a nice location, and it's right on the water."

"It's just a house, Alex, and I'm not attached to it. And if things don't work out between us, I'm not moving back into this house with all its sad memories. I plan on moving to Venice Beach where at least I'll be happy with my surroundings."

A few weeks later, he received some good news at work. His assignment was renewed and it would be another two years before he would have to return to his job in New Mexico. We continued to see each other several times a week and always enjoyed each other's company. Even though it felt like the relationship was growing, he continued to remain noncommittal. Whenever I told him that I loved him, he always told me the same thing, or something similar to it: "That's very good." There were a few times when I thought I heard him trying to say the words "I love you" to himself when he didn't know that I was listening to him. My thoughts were that perhaps he did love me, but he did not know how to say it.

In August of 2010, we went to a weekend dance event in St. Petersburg, Florida, sponsored by the Tampa Bay Beach Boppers. This was the second dancing weekend event we had attended together—the first one being in Nashville, Tennessee, the year before. Something special happened during the event in St. Petersburg which took our relationship to the next level. We arrived at our hotel on a hot summer's day in August, eager to learn new dance steps from the excellent teachers who were part of the program. Our favorites were Mike and Debbie LaPina from Chicago, Illinois. Our dancing friends Joy, Donna, Ray, and Dakota were also at the event, which made it even more enjoyable and fun. During the day we attended dance classes, and in the evenings we met our friends in the large ballroom for social dancing. On the first morning, we walked across the street to try a breakfast place that everyone was bragging about. They served an entire breakfast for only three dollars. As we passed by the cash register with our breakfast on our trays, Alex went first. They collected his money and then waved me through.

After we sat down, I told him, "This is such a great deal, paying only three dollars for breakfast."

Looking at me with a puzzled look on his face, he said, "I don't understand. They charged me over six dollars for my breakfast."

I could not stop laughing when I told him, "Didn't they tell you that you were also paying for my breakfast?"

On the first night of the dance, our friend Joy proudly showed everyone her brand new diamond engagement ring. Excited and happy for her, all the ladies in our small group jumped up and down, clapping and shouting "Yeahhhhh!"

On the second night of the event, I said the usual "I love you" to Alex before we went to sleep.

A few minutes later, somewhere between the state of being asleep and being awake, I thought I heard him say, "I think I love you too."

When I woke up the next morning, I asked him, "Was I dreaming last "Was I dreaming last night or did I hear you say that you loved me too?"

I was overjoyed when he replied, "Yes, you did!"

"Oh my God! That's wonderful to hear."

That night during the social dance, it was me that the girls were clapping for, excitedly jumping up and down and shouting "Yeahhhhh!"

With the holidays approaching, we scheduled another trip to Pennsylvania. This time the trip was for a happy occasion to spend Thanksgiving with his family. During this visit, there were several family members and friends who had new engagement rings to show off. As I looked at each beautiful ring, my heart ached as I longed for the day when I would have one of my own from Alex. The best part of the entire visit was the pizza party that his brother-in-law Gary arranged for us. An excellent chef, he prepared several delicious pizzas, each one of them made from fresh ingredients. He even made his own sauce and pizza dough. I watched him as he prepared each pizza, pounding the dough with his hands, flinging it into the air, carefully adding his homemade sauce, finishing it with a different mix of toppings from the one just prepared. I enjoyed eating the pizzas more than the Thanksgiving feast the following day. It was an enjoyable visit as we spent several hours with his family and close friends.

When we returned to Florida, it was back to our normal routine of doing all the things together that we loved. Even though I enjoyed the time that we spent together, and continued to feel his love in my heart, I wanted something more from the relationship. I wanted to know that he loved me enough to spend the rest of his life with me. And what I wanted most of all was for him to look deep into my eyes and say, "I love you, Lisa." I thought many times about asking him if he felt the same way. The reason I never asked is because I thought it would mean more to me if he told me on his own. I convinced myself that it just had to evolve and it would happen when the time was right.

During the month of December, I began to have problems with my muscles which were sore and aching most of the time. When I went to see my doctor about it, he advised me to consult with a massage therapist and schedule regular appointments. Remembering how good Della was the last time I had a session with her, I immediately began seeing her on a regular basis. She was magnificent. Besides massaging away all the aches and pains in my muscles, she also counseled me using her intuitive abilities. With each session, I began to feel better not only physically but also emotionally.

For the month of January, Alex and I flew to Texas to attend a wedding. His niece Sarah was getting married to the love of her life, Brandon, on the first day of January, 2011. The wedding was scheduled for one o'clock that afternoon at a Catholic church in the town of Tyler, Texas. The first two days that we were there, we spent time with his family and their friends. Even though we stayed at a local hotel, we spent several hours visiting at the house where his brother Steve and wife Cindi lived. A gorgeous brick house, I could sense the love that was shared in it the moment we walked through the front door. From looking at the décor in her house, it was obvious

189

that Cindi loved roosters. There were rooster lamps, rooster figurines, and anything else that could be made to look like a rooster. Since it was just after Christmas, there were beautiful holiday ornaments throughout the house. I especially loved all her Santa Claus figurines from different parts of the world.

The thing that I liked most about their house was the backyard. When I walked out their back door, there were steps made out of stones and pebbles which were part of a block wall. As I walked down the steps, I first looked up at the beautiful tall oak trees. There were also sweet gum trees, dogwoods, apple trees, and a crepe myrtle. As I walked amongst the many trees, I noticed several large ceramic frogs scattered throughout the yard. After sitting on the wooden swing that Steve had built, I strolled toward the perimeter of the property. Seeing an arched wooden bridge, built over a creek with no water, I just had to walk on it and even asked Alex to take my picture.

During our visits inside the house, we had wonderful conversations, shared good food together, and even played a few games of *Scrabble*. Just like the time when we visited his family in Pennsylvania, there were several young ladies showing off their new engagement rings. It tugged at my heart each time that I looked at one, still hoping for one of my own. When some of the women were comparing their rings, and we were sitting on the sofa, his sister Paula was kind enough to let me put her diamond ring on my finger. Alex was sitting on the other side of me when I showed it to him.

"Look honey, her ring fits me perfectly. She told me it's a size seven."

Looking slightly interested, he responded with, "Seven?"

The wedding ceremony was absolutely stunning. The bride had the most magnificent dress I had ever seen. She was wearing a Vera Wang strapless layered tulle gown. She was such a beautiful bride that she was featured on the front cover of *The Wedded Bliss* magazine in a cinematic 40s-inspired photo. During the wedding ceremony, Alex and I were sitting next to Paula when I noticed her whispering something into his ear.

Curious about what she had said, I asked him, "What did your sister just say to you?"

"She asked me if I was taking notes."

Acting like I did not know why she said that, I asked him, "Oh really. Why would she ask you that?"

"In case I ever decide to do this."

Thinking about his comment, it made me wonder whether or not he ever would decide, because it wasn't apparent by his actions.

When we returned home from the wedding, he suggested that we book a cruise during the month of April on one of the new ships out of Fort Lauderdale. I was especially excited about this cruise because this time it would just be the two of us, creating the perfect opportunity for romance, or perhaps even a marriage proposal. Since the ship's capacity was over 6,000 passengers, we had to make reservations for all our shows and dinners months before the cruise. When doing this, he chose one of the specialty restaurants so that we could have a romantic dinner together one evening. It gave me a ray of hope when he did this, making me think that something special may happen during that dinner.

In the coming months leading up to the cruise, I talked to my sister Gail, and most of my friends, about my excitement over a possible marriage proposal during the upcoming cruise. My gut feelings, which were telling me it was going to happen, were strong and were fueled even more by my excitement over the idea as I thought about it. Although most of my friends were receptive to my enthusiasm on the subject, and were happy that I shared it with them, I had one friend who was not. In a very stern voice, she told me that everyone knew, including me, that it was never going to happen. Although what she said to me was an obvious assumption, based on how noncommittal he had been; it was not what I felt in my heart and hurt me deeply when I heard her say it.

Feeling depressed about it, I called my sister Gail to have her console me. If it weren't for my sister's love and understanding, always encouraging me, I may have given up on Alex, thinking that a commitment from him may never happen. My sister knew me better than anyone else did. She thought the world of Alex, and was persistent with her reminders to me of how good she thought we were together. I was also thankful for my other friends who encouraged me and gave me love and understanding, especially the ones that I met through various dancing events. A few of my friends advised me to stop giving him hints all the time, which would allow him to make a decision on his own. Taking their advice, I did stop giving him hints, at least for a while, until we went on our cruise together.

The month of April finally arrived and I started packing my suitcase. On the night before the cruise, I went through my checklist and noticed that there were a few items missing that still needed to be packed. Not remembering where I put them when I unpacked the last time, I searched through my dresser drawers to find them. When I looked into the top drawer of my dresser, I discovered a little black velvet ring box. Even though I knew that the box was empty, I opened it. At that very moment, as I looked into the box, another beautiful feeling came over me. I could clearly envision a beautiful diamond ring, as if it were in the box that I was holding in my hands. I said to myself out loud, "Oh my God! It's beautiful!" Sometimes we have a distinct feeling of knowing when something is going to happen; this was one of those times.

(Chapter 17)

THE MORNING OF APRIL 2, 2011, finally arrived. Looking forward to a romantic cruise with just the two of us, I was filled with excitement as I packed the last few items into my suitcase. Although I had trouble sleeping the night before, my energy level remained high, fueled by my excitement. Alex and I were about to sail on one of the two largest ships in the world, the *Oasis of the Seas*. Its sister ship, the *Allure of the Seas*, was officially larger, but by only a few inches. After Alex arrived at my house and we loaded up our suitcases, we drove almost four hours before we arrived at Port Everglades in Fort Lauderdale. Even before we reached the entrance to the port, we could see our ship towering above all the others. We parked our vehicle, grabbed our suitcases, and walked across the street to the cruise terminal. As we walked toward the entrance to the terminal, we could not help staring at the gigantic ship in front of us. Eighteen decks high, it towered over the brand new cruise terminal in front of it. When we entered the terminal, we were overwhelmed at how organized it was, with all the latest technology available for speeding up the check-in process. Even though there were over 6,000 passengers boarding the ship, it took us less than ten minutes to check in and receive our boarding passes.

When we walked onto the ship on deck five, we were fascinated as we looked at our surroundings. As we walked through the Royal Promenade to explore, we discovered coffee shops which were perfect places for people-watching, restaurants where we could have lunch in the afternoons, and endless places for entertainment in the evenings. After discovering several restaurants to choose from for lunch, we decided on the Windjammer Café near the top of the ship. We filled our plates with the many choices of food that were offered at the buffet, and then chose a table next to a window which overlooked the basketball court on the deck below. As we ate our lunch, our attentions were drawn to the deck below where we watched an energetic group of young men shooting baskets. Watching them play brought back memories of my mother who loved to play basketball.

After lunch we decided to explore the ship and check out all the other decks. We began on deck six and toured the spa and fitness center. Every cruise that I take, I always tour the spa first because it makes me feel more relaxed and helps with the transition into vacation mode. As we walked through the treatment rooms, they explained the different massages and body wraps that they offered. My favorite part of the tour was when they demonstrated the hot stone treatment by giving us a mini massage. As we felt the warmth of the hot stones on our shoulders, we wished that we were one of the models receiving treatments on the massage tables. Then we checked out the fitness center to see what type of equipment they had.

After our tour of the spa and fitness center, we made our way to our balcony cabin on the eleventh deck. Looking out our balcony we had a magnificent view of Central Park. Offering a touch of Manhattan, the park was located at the center of the ship on deck eight. It quickly became our favorite part of the ship. Beautifully landscaped with tropical foliage and seasonal flowers, it was the perfect place for relaxing, shopping, fine-dining, or just taking a stroll. Later on in our cruise, whenever we had enough of the hustle and bustle of the crowds, I would say to Alex, "Honey, would you like to take a walk in the park?" It was so peaceful when we went to the park that we almost forgot we were on a busy cruise ship. As we walked on the serene winding pathways, leading us through lush tropical grounds, we could smell the sweet fragrance from the flower gardens, look up at the tropical plants on the trellises above us, and feel the coolness when we walked through the shady areas created by the canopy of trees above us.

Exhausted from all the activities of the afternoon, we rested for a few hours until it was time for our first dinner experience on the ship. Having the option of sitting at a different table each night in the main dining room, we were able to meet new people each time that we dined. We had a fun conversation with the first group of dinner guests we sat with. More than once during our conversation, they told us that Alex and I should get married. Each time that the subject came up, I commented that it would be wonderful, but Alex just smiled and said nothing. After dinner, we took a walk over to the boardwalk area to do some more exploring.

A taste of Coney Island, the Boardwalk offered many of the same attractions that you would find at a seaside park—traditional carnival games, a psychic and tattoo parlor, an ice cream parlor, a candy shop with cotton candy, and several open-aired restaurants. The only activity that interested me was riding on the old fashioned carousel. The carousel had twenty-one figures handcrafted out of poplar wood, to include horses, zebras, lions, and giraffes. When we rode on the carousel together, we felt like young children spending the day at a park. Shortly after leaving the carousel, we heard live music playing in the background. We looked toward the back of the ship and discovered a show in progress not far from where we were standing. What we saw was the enormous Aqua Theater with a swimming pool that had diving boards several feet above it. The seating area was full, but we had a perfect view of the show from where we stood, right behind the last row of seats. We watched in amazement as several divers, synchronized swimmers, and acrobats performed water ballets, acrobatic feats, and Olympic-type dives—all choreographed to beautiful music and a light show. It was simply amazing! At one point during the show, several performers dived into the pool, and seconds later, the bottom of the pool was raised to the top as they all came out of the water standing up.

After the show, we left that area of the ship and headed toward the promenade, which was the heartbeat of the ship. When we heard salsa music playing at one of the bars, we stopped to take a look and noticed two dance instructors on the floor doing a striking salsa dance together. After watching them and listening to a few more songs, we decided to dance the Cha Cha. Even though we were wearing sandals, because our dance shoes were still in the cabin, we did a great job and received a small applause from the few spectators who were watching us. We then checked out some of the stores but I could not coax Alex to go into the fine jewelry store with me. After walking through all the other stores in the promenade, we headed over to Central Park again, located three decks above the promenade.

It was peaceful walking amongst the many trees and plants, listening to the sounds of birds chirping in the background. When we looked up, we realized something unique that we had never seen before on a cruise ship. There was no ceiling on that part of the ship and we could see the stars. Even though we were on a cruise ship, it was a remarkable feeling when we realized that we were walking outside in a park, and there were stars shining down on us from above. When we strolled past the art gallery, we noticed some beautiful works of art that caught our attention. Curious to learn more about the artist who painted them, we walked into the gallery. We discovered that his name was Viktor Shvaiko, a famous artist from Russia who was vacationing on board the ship with his family. His paintings were magnificent—original oils and prints of café scenes from Italy and France, showing similarities to the works of Thomas Kincaid, evidenced by the light that he painted into the scenes. We were given a brief history of the artist and learned that he would be doing live painting demonstrations throughout the cruise. We took note of it, and looked forward to watching him paint. Before leaving the gallery, the manager approached us and added more to what he had already told us about the artist. He shared a fascinating story about how he began his career in art. During the time that he and his wife lived in Ukraine, she wanted an original work of art but knew that they could never afford one. Viktor came home one day and surprised her by unveiling before her a magnificent original oil painting.

After seeing the painting, she asked him, "How could you ever afford such a beautiful work of art?"

When he told her he had painted it himself, she became active in motivating him to change his line of work. Overcoming many challenges, he eventually became a successful artist in New York where his paintings earned the interest and admiration of collectors from around the world.

After everything we had done on our first day of cruising, we were completely exhausted. Calling it a day, we headed back to our cabin for a good night's sleep. On the way to the cabin we passed by the ship's library, and decided to stop and check it out. While I searched to see if they had a *Scrabble* game anywhere, Alex scanned the shelves searching for any books that would be of interest to him. Spotting one that he found interesting, he pulled it off the shelf.

Holding the book in his hand, laughing with a light chuckle, he looked at me and said, "Hey, check this out."

I glanced at the book that he had in his hand, and gave him a sigh as I said, "That's an interesting book, Alex. Are you planning on reading it?"

The book was titled "Lessons for Husbands." I felt a twinge of hope in my heart, wondering if there was a possibility that he may propose to me at some point during the cruise. Filled with excitement and anticipation, I happily looked forward to the events that would unfold during the next seven days.

Morning arrived with thoughts of where to eat breakfast—the main dining room or the buffet. After deciding that we wanted a little pampering, we chose the main dining room over the buffet, thinking about the impeccable service that comes with every meal served in the dining room. We were seated with a couple of doctors from Los Angeles and enjoyed an interesting conversation with them during our meal. Like most people that Alex and I meet when we're together, they automatically assumed that we were married.

After breakfast, we decided to get some exercise, and set a goal of walking five laps around the ship's jogging path—a total of two miles. We started out at a normal pace, working our way up to a brisk walk, occasionally jogging around anyone walking at a slower pace. Not paying attention during one of these jogs, I caught my shoe on one of the door entrances, causing me to lose my balance, helplessly tumbling forward, ending up face down on the deck—happy that I did not break my sunglasses in the process. Within seconds, I was approached by a ship employee who asked me if I was OK. Feeling a little more embarrassed than injured, I stood up and continued on the jogging path, as if it had never happened.

After our adventurous exercise routine, we explored more of the ship, taking several photographs with my new fancy digital camera. We watched the welcome aboard parade in the promenade, and then had lunch at the Solarium Bistro. It was advertised as being the healthiest place to eat on the ship with all meals being five hundred calories or less. Some of the healthy food choices were black eyed peas, red cabbage with apples, brown rice, and carrots with raisins and walnuts. The ship provided so many choices for places to eat that we were able to try a new restaurant each day of the cruise. Some of the restaurants were so good that we ended up eating at them more than once. There were many activities on board the ship to keep us busy, including a Broadway version of *Hair Spray* and a beautifully choreographed ice show with Olympic skaters in elaborate costumes. One of my favorite shows was their headliner show featuring a band called "Beatlemania." They looked and sounded exactly like the Beatles—my favorite band while I was growing up. While watching the show, I thought about the first time that I heard the Beatles sing when I was only ten years old. The entire family was sitting in the living room watching the Ed Sullivan show. When the Beatles were introduced by Ed Sullivan to the television audience, my father made the comment, "They must be comedians; look at how long their hair is."

One of our favorite events that we attended was the live painting demonstration by Viktor Shvaiko, which took place in Central Park during the evening. We watched as he sat in front of his easel, dipping his brushes into his painter's pallet, expertly applying oils to his canvas, unveiling a beautiful café scene from Italy. He painted in many layers, showing the season and time of day by adding details to the top layer, diligently painting flowers and then shadows. In the background, we could hear soft guitar music being played by one of the ship's musicians. There was a young boy in the audience who caught my attention. I watched him as he sat on the edge of his seat, holding on to his sketch pad, watching the artist paint. He was obviously a young artist with hopes and dreams of being as good as the painter he was observing.

Watching this scene brought back memories from my childhood when I watched my brother Billy paint. A gifted artist, he painted several oil paintings when he was still a young boy. He was so good that the teachers where he attended elementary school had fights amongst themselves over whose classroom he would be in. I loved sitting in the chair as I watched him first sketch out a beautiful nature scene in pencil, and then carefully add the oils with his brush, one layer at a time, similar to the way that Viktor was painting. My parents bragged about him all the time, telling everyone about the many local judged art competitions and prestigious awards that he won. Some of his paintings were featured in touring exhibitions that went all over the country, including the Hallmark Cards tour. When he grew up, he followed his passion for painting and worked full-time as a successful art teacher in the public school system where he taught in several county middle schools until he retired. After retiring from his teaching career, he used his artistic abilities to change his part-time job as a videographer into a full-time job as a special events videographer, winning many local and international awards.

On the third day of the cruise, I finally persuaded Alex to go into the fine jewelry store with me. Keeping to his normal routine, he immediately walked over to where the watches were while I headed over to look at the diamond rings. I was beginning to wonder if he would ever find a watch that he liked. While looking at the diamonds, I asked the saleswoman if I could try on a few rings. I told her that I had a hunch that my boyfriend (who was in the store looking at watches) may decide to propose marriage to me during the cruise. In the jeweler's case there were several blue diamond rings on display. After asking about them, she explained that a natural blue diamond is a rare and expensive stone, and then further explained the process of changing a diamond's color to blue. The treatment can only work with a small amount of diamonds, which have to be of a certain quality. They are irradiated first—causing the color to change—followed by a heat treatment to stabilize the color. I told her that my father proposed to my mother by giving her a natural blue diamond back in the 1940s.

After trying on one of the rings, I waved at Alex and said, "Honey, please come look at this ring. It's a really nice blue diamond."

He walked toward me to take a quick look at it, and said, "Yes, that is a nice ring, Lisa."

"Did I ever tell you that my father gave my mother a blue diamond ring when he proposed to her, although hers was a completely natural blue diamond?"

"Yes, I think you did tell me that at least once, if not more."

As he walked away to return to the watches, I sadly told the woman, "Thank you for showing me this beautiful ring. I don't think we'll be buying one today."

My thoughts, as we were leaving the store, were either he was not ready for a commitment, or on a more positive note, perhaps he had already bought me a ring and was planning to surprise me at dinner one night during the cruise.

Knowing that I loved playing the slot machines, the next day after dinner Alex suggested that we go to the casino. Once I chose a machine and sat down to play it, he handed me a few dollars, telling me, "Why don't you wait right here while I go to the gym to do a workout. It shouldn't take me more than an hour and then I'll be back." I happily accepted his offer. Sitting there alone, I began thinking about my mother and how much she loved to play the machines. My sister Gail received a reading once from psychic medium John Edward where he talked about my mother in reference to a slot machine. He said that she was not strong enough to come through during the reading, but if they had slot machines in Heaven, that is where she would be hanging out. After about two hours, I became a little concerned and wondered why Alex had not returned yet. Changing my thoughts to something more positive, I thought perhaps he went back to the jewelry store that we visited the day before.

When he finally returned, we left the casino and took a stroll through the promenade, walking past the shops. As we walked by the jewelry store, I noticed the woman who had shown me the blue diamond rings the night before. She was standing just outside the store's entrance. I thought it interesting that she was smiling as we walked by, and then she winked at Alex.

I had to ask him, "Did you see how that woman was smiling at you?"

"Well, that's not surprising. We did look at some diamonds with her yesterday."

With nothing else being said, we continued our walk down the promenade. Thinking about what just happened; thoughts began racing through my head as to why she did that: Was he at the gym the entire time that I was in the casino? Or did he go to the gym first and then the jewelry store to talk to her about diamonds? Did he maybe even buy the ring that I picked out? When we initially booked our cruise, he insisted on booking at least one night in one of the specialty restaurants, telling me it would be a special dinner. Maybe, just maybe he was going to finally pop the long-awaited question, asking me to marry him. When we reached the end of the promenade, he casually walked over to the shopping guide's booth to pick up some coupons. I wasn't at all surprised when he did this. Regardless of wherever we went shopping, he always had a coupon for that particular store. The woman handed him a few coupons, the only one catching my eye being the one for Diamonds International. After asking her where to go in Cozumel for the best shopping, she told us to make sure that the taxi driver dropped us off at the Forum shops, which is where all the best stores were. Alex listened carefully to her as he slipped the coupons into his pocket. Even though he loved coupons, we had already received more than enough in our cabin and had to throw most of them away. I automatically assumed that the coupons he just received would also be thrown away.

The next day was a wonderful, relaxing day at sea. Having cruised many times before, those are the days that I look forward to the most. You are able to sleep in as late as you want without the worry of being anywhere at a particular time. Then you have the entire day to enjoy the ship, picking and choosing the activities that you want to do—or just relaxing all day by the pools or in the whirlpools. This was the day that we had our special dinner reserved in Chops Grille, one of the fine-dining restaurants on the ship. I was planning on wearing the prettiest dress that I had and Alex was going to wear a suit and tie.

Thinking all day about the possibility of a marriage proposal at dinner, I kept envisioning what I thought it would be like. Would he kneel down on one knee, or would he surprise me by putting the ring on my dinner plate? The possibilities that I thought about were endless. Almost three years since the day we met, two people in love sharing a romantic dinner for two would be the perfect setting for a marriage proposal.

As I slipped into the special dress that I had packed for the occasion, it was almost time for our dinner reservation. The dress was a stunning, royal blue Adrianna Papell with silver beads around the waist and a full skirt with rosette blooms at the bottom. I had bought it at Macy's for our second Valentine's dinner—the last time that I thought he would propose to me. On that day, I was excited about the possibility of an engagement. When we got to the restaurant, I quietly whispered to the hostess, "My boyfriend may be surprising me with an engagement ring during dinner."

Sorely disappointed when I left the restaurant without one, I said to myself: Maybe next time it will happen.

All dressed and ready to go, I looked at Alex and noticed how handsome he looked wearing his new suit. Then he asked me, "Well, are you ready for our special dinner, Lisa?"

"Yes! I'm looking forward to our romantic evening together. I'm wearing a special dress for the occasion."

"Wow. You look stunningly beautiful in that dress."

The restaurant was located on my favorite part of the ship, Central Park. Walking through the park at night was delightful with the tiny white lights flickering in all the palm trees. When we entered the restaurant, we were greeted by the manager who showed us to our table. Sitting at the table looking at Alex, I told him: "This is a nice restaurant; it has such a romantic atmosphere. Thank you for taking me to dinner here this evening."

"You're welcome, Lisa."

Before ordering our dinner, he asked the waiter to bring us two of the special martinis of the day so that we could have a toast. When the waiter brought our drinks to the table, he asked us, "Are the two of you celebrating anything special this evening?"

Looking at Alex, expecting him to say something romantic, I was disappointed when he said, "No. There isn't any special occasion. It's just the two of us having a wonderful dinner together."

Feeling a little upset, I did the best that I could to maintain my composure, still hoping that something romantic would happen. As we raised our glasses, I looked into his eyes, still feeling a shimmer of hope. Looking back at me, with a smile on his face, he said, "This is to having a wonderful cruise together and a wonderful dinner."

Again, I thought to myself: Maybe next time it will happen. Thinking about more cheerful things, like eating, I picked up the menu to order my dinner. Since it was the most perfect opportunity for him to propose to me, and he didn't, I no longer had any expectations that it would happen during the cruise. Deciding to forget about it for a while, I thought about the fun things we would be doing together during the next few days.

Day five arrived as the ship pulled into the port of Cozumel, Mexico. A small island that lies just off the coast of Mexico's Yucatan peninsula, it is known for its spectacular coral reefs and turquoise blue waters. It is also known for its combination of upscale and funky shops in the downtown tourist district. The only purchase I was planning on making during our stop was a pretty blue and white tequila bottle. Even though I was not a big fan of tequila, I fell in love with some of the beautiful ceramic bottles of tequila that I saw during our last trip to Cozumel. When we disembarked from the ship and walked onto the pier, we were amazed at how much it had changed since the last time we were there. It was obvious they had done some major renovations, possibly due to hurricane damage. There were several duty free shops located near the dock, which made it convenient for anyone who did not want to venture out too far from the ship. Since we did want to venture out and explore the shops in the downtown district, we searched for a taxi to take us downtown.

After climbing into our taxi, we gave the driver clear instructions to take us to the Forum Shops. The ride into town, as he drove along the shoreline, was beautiful with a magnificent view of the turquoise blue Caribbean water. Once we reached the center of the downtown area, the taxi driver stopped his vehicle and told us we had reached our destination.

Not being able to see the Forum shops, Alex asked the taxi driver, "Could you please tell us where the Forum shops are? I don't see them anywhere."

Speaking with the best English he could, the driver told Alex, "You are very close. They are only two blocks away."

After we walked several blocks in the hot Mexican sun, we realized that the taxi driver was a little misleading on how far away we actually were from our destination. I assumed that he wanted us to check out some of the local vendors before we reached the big shops.

During our walk, Alex asked me, "Is there anything special as far as jewelry that you would like me to buy for you while we're in Cozumel?"

Too disappointed to bring up diamonds again, I quickly told him: "No. The only thing that I want to buy on this trip is one of those pretty ceramic bottles that tequila comes in. I think I already have enough jewelry."

Thinking back to the last time when we were in Cozumel, I remembered the beautiful necklace that he bought for me in one of the silver shops. Just like the time before when he bought me diamond earrings in St Thomas, he loved watching me stroll through the store as I picked out several pieces of jewelry to try on. Once I found something that he thought I liked, he would ask me, "Do you like that piece of jewelry?" If I said yes, he would always buy it for me. He told me later on that it made it easier for him to buy me something once he knew for sure that I liked it. As we continued to walk toward the Forum Shops, we stopped in a few of the stores but did not spend much time in any of them. We were looking forward to shopping where we would find larger stores with more merchandise to choose from.

After walking for what seemed like miles, we finally arrived at the Forum Shops. The entrance to the shops led us directly into the largest Diamonds International store I had ever seen. There were jewelry counters everywhere with every type of stone you could possibly imagine. Since we had been walking for several blocks in the hot Mexican sun, we decided to freshen up a bit and took the escalator to the second floor where the restrooms were. On the second floor, they also had a pharmacy as well as an area where you could watch jewelry being designed. While we were riding back down the escalator, an idea suddenly popped into my head which came out of nowhere—almost as if it were not my own idea. Even though it was a bold and direct question, something in my gut told me that I just had to ask it.

Holding onto Alex's hand, I told him: "They have a lot of diamonds in this store. Would it be OK with you if we looked at some of them together? That way I can show you exactly what I like—just in case you ever decide to buy me one."

I was pleasantly surprised, and almost shocked, when he answered, "OK. We can do that."

My heart was beating a little louder as we arrived on the first floor and headed over to the diamond counter. We were greeted immediately by a salesman who was eager to assist us. After I asked him to educate my boyfriend about diamonds, he showed us a chart and explained everything there is to know about them—cut, clarity, color, and carat size.

As we were looking at the chart, I told the salesman, "I really like the princess cut diamonds. They are beautiful. May we look at some of those?"

He immediately reached into the glass case, pulled out four loose stones, and placed them on a velvet cloth so we could take a closer look. After he explained the differences in their qualities, he asked me to choose the one that I liked the best.

Looking at four gorgeous stones, I thought about it for only a few seconds before I said, "Of course I like the shiny one the best!"

Then the salesman reached into the glass case again and picked out a beautiful setting for the stone. The setting that he picked was made out of 18-carat white gold with eight additional diamonds, four on each side. In the middle of the eight diamonds were the prongs where my diamond would go. He carefully picked up the diamond I had chosen, and placed it on top of the setting, showing us how they would look together. It was strikingly beautiful, looking almost like the ring I had envisioned in the empty black box the night before our cruise.

Very excited, I looked at Alex and said, "Are you learning anything here?"

"Yes . . . I am learning that you want a diamond ring really bad."

Having the perfect opportunity to tell him something that I had wanted to say for a couple of years, I answered him. "It's not just the ring that I want—but what it stands for. What I really want from you is a commitment." It felt really good when I said it.

The salesman then took the setting, with the loose stone cradled on top of it, and slid it onto my finger. I looked at Alex again, and asked him what he thought. He said nothing.

Disappointed again, and almost in tears, I looked at the salesman and said, "I don't think he's ready for this yet. We may as well leave."

Before we could walk away, another salesman in a white jacket suddenly appeared behind the counter, and asked us if he could be of assistance.

With Alex still being quiet, I told the salesman, "I'm sorry, we were just leaving. We did look at some diamonds, and they are all beautiful, but I don't think we're going to buy one today."

The guy in the white jacket looked me straight in the eyes and told me with indisputable certainty, "Don't you worry, miss. I will make sure you have a ring on your finger today before you leave this store!"

I was surprised by what he said, thinking that Alex must be shaking in his shoes just from hearing it. The salesman looked at Alex and then looked at me again, asking us if we would like to look at some smaller diamonds that would be less expensive.

Not hesitating for even a second, I immediately said, "No . . . I would like to get a price on this ring . . . just to see how much it is."

He took out his calculator and came up with various prices, watching the expressions on our faces for when he thought we were happy with his figures. Once he settled on the final price for the ring, Alex finally spoke up.

Looking at me and the ring I was wearing, he quietly asked me, "Do you like this ring?"

Feeling a beautiful sense of peace, joy, and relief, I looked at Alex and said, "Yes! I love this ring!"

With a smile on his face, he said, "OK."

I gave him a huge hug as I told him, "We're getting engaged!"

Quickly responding to me, he said, "Yes, we are."

It was such a beautiful moment. I felt like I was in shock and wanted to pinch myself to make sure that I wasn't dreaming.

Then the salesman asked him something that surprised me when I heard him say it. "Sir, do you have the coupon with you from the shopping guide on the ship so that we can apply the discount?"

To my complete surprise and total amazement, he said, "Yes, I do," as he slowly reached into his pocket and pulled out the coupon given to him by the woman in the promenade—just after we left the casino. It suddenly hit me that the entire event may have been masterfully planned, down to the last detail. Thinking back, I thought about the woman in the jewelry store who smiled at him when we walked past her. He must have gone to see her for advice as to where to purchase a diamond ring—and also where to find a coupon—doing it all while

I was waiting in the casino for his return, wondering at the time why his workout at the gym was taking so long.

Since it would take over an hour for them to set the ring, they recommended we go next door to Pancho's Backyard for lunch and margaritas. Located in a lovely courtyard, the restaurant had a charming atmosphere.

After we sat down at the table, I had to ask him, "Is getting engaged something you had been thinking about?"

"Yes, for about two months now. You made it really easy for me today."

Then he asked me, "Do you feel any different?"

"Yes, I feel happy! How about you, how do you feel right now?"

Looking at me with a smile on his face, he said, "I am more relaxed now."

As we ate a delicious Mexican meal and sipped on our margaritas, we were serenaded by two musicians playing the Marimbas. After we talked for a while, we headed back to the store to pick up the ring. After we entered the store, we were greeted by one of the other salesmen.

"Hello! We have been expecting the two of you. Welcome back to our store. It'll be a few minutes before your ring is ready. We would like you to wait over there in the diamond section."

Not surprising to me, Alex headed in the direction of the watches while I strolled over to the diamond section. After a few short minutes, the man in the white jacket approached me.

"Would you care to go upstairs with me? I would like to show you something." As we were riding up the escalator, he told me about the factory upstairs where they design jewelry. When we reached the second floor, he walked me over to the glass wall where we could see the jewelry design area behind it. He showed me one of the craftsmen making a new piece of jewelry, telling me that they do it first in silver and then redo it in gold. Interrupted by a phone call, he left for a moment.

Upon returning, he told me, "While we're up here, let's check on your ring to see if it's ready yet." After looking at a chart, he said, "Let's go. Your ring is ready and waiting for you downstairs."

Riding down the escalator with him, overjoyed about putting the ring on my finger, I saw Alex. He was standing proudly at the bottom of the escalator. He had a huge smile on his face and was holding the little black ring box in his hand.

As I walked up to him, he opened it, quietly telling me, "Here it is."

Inside the black velvet box, I saw my beautiful new engagement ring. He took it out of the box and gently placed it on my finger. Still in shock, but unbelievably happy, I threw my arms around him and gave him a huge kiss.

When I finished hugging him and looked up at him, I said, "We're engaged!"

With a smile on his face, he answered me, "Yes, we are! And we're going to be married."

Once we arrived back on the ship, I was ecstatic and wanted to tell everyone about my new engagement ring. While we were riding in the elevator, Alex asked me: "What are you going to do, Lisa? You won't be able to tell anyone about your ring for two more days."

Smiling as I answered him, I said, "Are you kidding me? I don't need to wait until after the cruise. There are over six thousand people on this ship who have not seen my ring."

Everywhere we went on the ship, I proudly showed off my new ring, bringing it up in conversation every time that we went on the elevator or met someone new while we were eating. As I walked down the promenade, it felt as if my feet were not even touching the floor. I was absolutely in love with him and was thrilled with the idea of spending the rest of my life with him.

When we arrived back home after the cruise, the first person that I wanted to show my ring to was my dear friend Lorraine. When I drove to her house and pulled into her driveway, Donny was standing in the driveway next to his van. As I stepped out of my vehicle to walk toward the front door, I became increasingly aware of the ring that was on my finger, not knowing how he would feel if he saw it. As I walked by him, I casually said hello and kept on going.

I was surprised when he answered me and said, "Hi, Lisa! How was your cruise?"

Before I could even begin to think about what to say to him, I instinctively showed him my left hand and said, "Look at what I got on the cruise!"

As he looked at the ring on my finger, I was expecting him to be upset by what I had just told him. Instead, his response touched my heart; he also knew that real love is when the other person's happiness is more important than your own. And I realized with certainty that I had found my true match in Alex.

"Wow! That is a beautiful ring, Lisa. At least now I know that you will be happy."

And I'm certain I will.

~ THE END ~

Resources

Heathkit Education Systems - www.heathkit.com

Fractal Time: The Secret of 2012 and a New World Age. Gregg Braden, Hay House, Inc.
www.greggbraden.com

E-8C Joint STARS - www.as.northropgrumman.com/products/e8cjointstars/index.html

E-3 AWACS Overview - www.boeing.com/defense-space/ic/awacs/index.html

Mark Desrochers, Singer Guitarist - www.singerguitarist.com

Desrochers Video Productions - www.marylandvideographer.com

Gordon Smith, Psychic Medium - www.gordonsmithmedium.com

John Holland, Psychic Medium - www.johnholland.com

John Edward, Psychic Medium - www.johnedward.net

John Rogers - www.themediumwithin.com

Hazel West Burley, Spiritualist Medium Counselor - www.hazelburley.com
P.O. Box 92
1270 Clark St., Cassadaga, FL 32706
(386) 228-3826

Della Danley, Licensed Massage Therapist and Intuitive Counselor - (321) 768-7575

Tampa Bay Beach Boppers - www.tampabaybeachboppers.com

Information for Contra Dancing in Florida - www.dancefl.us

Information for Viktor Shvaiko Paintings - www.viktorshvaiko.com

Steve Cook, Remodeling Specialist - (321) 431-1917

Hay House, Inc. - www.hayhouse.com

Made in the USA
Lexington, KY
17 January 2012